What readers
Viking Ma

'I loved *Runestone*
they are both soo

'Your latest boo
Matthews family

'Your first two books were amazing, I couldn't believe
how real they felt. I finished reading them in two days.'
Kathryn

'Hurry up with the third book please.' Ben

'Highly recommended.' *Magpies*

'Another winner.' www.aussiereviews.com

As a child, ANNA CIDDOR loved reading, drawing and writing, but she never dreamed of becoming an author and illustrator. It was only when she married and had children of her own that the idea first crossed her mind. In 1987 she decided to take a break from her teaching career and 'have a go' at writing a book. The teaching career has been on hold ever since! Anna is now a full-time writer and illustrator, with over 50 titles published. She based the stories of *Runestone*, *Wolfspell* and *Stormriders* on research into real Viking lifestyle and beliefs.

Anna lives in Melbourne, Australia, with her husband and two children.

In 2003, *Runestone* was chosen as a Children's Book Council of Australia Notable Book and shortlisted for several Children's Choice Book Awards.

To find out more about Vikings and the background to the Viking Magic series, go to:

www.viking-magic.com

stormriders

The third book about
the adventures of
Oddo and Thora

ANNA CIDDOR

ALLEN&UNWIN

First published in 2004

Copyright © text and illustrations, Anna Ciddor, 2004

First distributed in the United States of America in 2007 by
Independent Publishers Group Inc., Chicago

Allen & Unwin
83 Alexander Street
Crows Nest NSW 2065
Australia
Phone: (61 2) 8425 0100
Fax: (61 2) 9906 2218
Email: info@allenandunwin.com
Web: www.allenandunwin.com

National Library of Australia
Cataloguing-in-Publication entry:

Ciddor, Anna
Stormriders: the third book about the adventures of
Oddo and Thora

For children.
ISBN 978 1 74114 360 7

1. Title. (Series: Ciddor, Anna. Viking magic; bk.3).

A823.3

Designed by Jo Hunt
Set in 12.5 pt Bembo by Midland Typesetters
Printed by McPherson's Printing Group, Maryborough

3 5 7 9 10 8 6 4 2

Teaching notes for *Stormriders* are available
on the Allen & Unwin website: www.allenandunwin.com

Secret rune messages

Runes are the letters of the Viking alphabet
(the Futhark).
Runes also have magic powers.
If you unlock the secrets of the rune messages in this
book you will find out *how to make your own*

(the Futhark at the end of the book
will probably come in handy).

Thank you to all the wonderful people who helped me create *Stormriders*.

Thank you
to my special readers Hannah and Yianni, Jemima and Miranda, Sophie and Elissa
to my inspirational editors Sarah Brenan and Rosalind Price
to my sister Tamar who always helps me find the wood among the trees
to Dennis King for his advice on Old Irish
to my incredible husband Gary for his enthusiasm and valuable suggestions
and
to the grade 5 class at Grimwade House, Melbourne Grammar, who loved my first unpublished draft of *Runestone* and gave me the confidence to finish writing the series!

Anna Ciddor
Melbourne, January 2004

Contents

1 Invaders!   9

2 Grimmr's thrall   12

3 The Sheriff's return   17

4 Encounter in the wood   22

5 A fine curach   27

6 A basket full of holes   34

7 Around the firepit   38

8 Oddo's dilemma   44

9 Which way?   50

10 Shape-change   59

11 The cauldron   64

12 Storm   71

13 Shipwreck   77

14 Ice and fire   82

15 The cave   88

16 The light in the rock   93

17 Search   96

18 Father Connlae   104

19 Goatskin   110

20 Under the hood   116

21	The plan	122
22	*Striker*	127
23	Unmasked	134
24	A gift for the King	140
25	Prisoners	144
26	The black horse	149
27	Lugnasad	155
28	A bargain with the King	160
29	Hurry!	166
30	Treasure	170
31	*Stormrider*	177
32	Gyda's secret	188

1
Invaders!

Dúngal hoisted up his tunic, tightened his girdle, and waded into the river. The surface of the water sparkled and danced. He squinted as he scanned its sandy bottom for smooth, round pebbles to use in his slingshot.

From behind him came the splash of oars. There was a *thud* as a curach drew up to the bank. Dúngal waited for someone to call out a greeting, but there was only the scrunch of feet and the clink of metal. Puzzled, he turned to look.

That was no curach. It was a huge longship, made of wood, and the men leaping onto the bank were carrying spears and daggers. Vikings!

One of them shouted in his strange language and pointed at Dúngal. His head, in its iron helmet, was like an evil grey skull. Dúngal tore the slingshot from his girdle, and felt round frantically in the water for a stone. Any stone. He fitted it to his slingshot, and fired.

It plopped pathetically at the Viking's feet.

The man gave a snort of laughter. His mouth was blood-red and his teeth gleamed. Dúngal splashed towards the bank and scrambled out of the water. His wet feet slithered on moss as he darted between the trees. He could hear Vikings crashing after him through the bracken.

The ringfort lay ahead, just across the field. Dúngal could see the deep ring of the ditch and the high earth wall. He just had to cross that ditch. Then he could pull up the wooden ramp and leave the invaders on the other side. Then he'd be safe with all his kinsfolk. Safe in the cobbled yard, with the little round house and the pointy roof, safe with his father and mother, sisters and brothers . . .

Two of his kinsmen were working in the field. They looked up, dropped tools, and broke into a run. Dúngal glanced over his shoulder. Pursuers were erupting from the trees, their spears glinting. He heard a rattle of wood as his kinsmen leapt onto the ramp and galloped across the ditch. Dúngal grabbed a discarded hoe and hurled it at the Vikings. One of them tripped, bellowing as he fell, and two other raiders somersaulted over him in a flurry of arms and legs.

'Yes!' cheered Dúngal.

But the next moment, a huge fist punched him in the back and sent him sprawling. His chin crashed into the earth, his teeth snapped against his tongue. He struggled to his knees, gasping for breath. His mouth tasted of blood. In the gateway ahead of him he saw his kinsmen bending to lift up the ramp.

'Wait!' yelled Dúngal. 'Wait for me!'

A hand seized him by the ankle, and dragged him backwards. He twisted, and thrashed wildly with his legs, trying to break free.

'Let me go, you big smelly marauder!'

His head bumped up and down as he was scraped over furrows and tree roots. Then the Viking ship loomed over him, its carved dragonhead leering down.

'No-o-o!'

The raider loosed his hold and Dúngal sprang to his feet. But as he turned to flee, the man grabbed him by the tunic. For an instant, Dúngal hung, legs flailing, then the Viking swung round and let go. Dúngal felt himself flying through the air, and the last thing he saw as he hurtled downwards was the wooden deck of the ship.

ᚦᛟᚱᚠ ᛏᛗᛁᛋ ᛟᛄᛟ

2
Grimmr's thrall

'Hey, Hairydog, would you like another dog to play with?'
Oddo bent down to pluck a curled-up leaf. 'This looks
just like your tail. And these,' he picked up a handful of
sticks, 'could be legs. Now, we just need a body, and a
head . . .' He gathered a few more leaves and twigs and
arranged them in the shape of a dog. 'I wonder if these
are the right plants for magic. Thora would know.'

He sat back on his heels and frowned at the pattern
he'd made on the ground. 'Do you think it looks like
a dog?' He glanced at Hairydog, who was watching
intently, head on one side. She seemed to raise an
eyebrow.

'Well, let's give it a try.' Oddo drew a deep breath and
began to chant.

'Where only leaf or twig now lies
Make a living dog arise!'

He grinned at Hairydog and waited. Hairydog poked her nose forward.

The curly leaf twitched and began to wag like a tail, and suddenly a little dog stumbled to its feet. It gave an excited yap and tried to run, but its legs were all different lengths and it toppled over. When Hairydog bent to sniff the fallen dog, there was nothing in front of her but a heap of leaves and twigs.

Oddo chuckled.

'I don't think I did that quite right,' he said. 'Oh well.'

'Oddo!' There was a shout, and Bolverk came striding across the ploughed field.

'Whoops. Better get back to work.' Oddo grabbed the basket of seed. His father would not be impressed to see him wasting his time on useless spells. Bolverk whistled, and Hairydog raced to meet him.

'That dog can make herself useful for a change,' called Bolverk. He jerked his head at the mountain pastures. 'She can help me check on the lambs.'

Oddo felt his father watching him as he set off down the line of furrows, carefully scattering a handful of grain with every second step.

'You look after those seeds,' said Bolverk, 'just the way you did last year, and we'll have the best crop in the district again. That greedy neighbour of ours will drool with envy.' Rubbing his hands, he turned towards the mountain.

Oddo straightened his shoulders. He looked at the ploughed rows of earth steaming gently in the spring sunshine, and pictured them covered with a fuzz of green shoots.

'All thanks to me,' he thought.

As he trod proudly forward, he glanced at Grimmr's farm on the other side of the fence. Working on the rocky strip of ground was a boy about his own age. Oddo had never seen him before.

'Must be a thrall,' thought Oddo. 'I bet Grimmr bought him at the market to do his dirty work. I don't envy him, working for that bully!'

The boy was struggling to up-end a heavy bucket. Dung poured out, and he began to spread it over the field. Oddo wrinkled his nose, dumped his basket on the ground and flapped his hands.

'Send me some wind,' he called to the sky. 'Blow this smell away!'

Immediately, a breeze sprang up and the odour faded. Oddo grinned and bent to retrieve his basket.

A young starling was perched on the edge, pecking at the seeds. 'Hey! What are you up to? I left some over there for you birds.' He pointed across the field to where a cluster of other birds was squabbling over a heap of barley. He looked at the thrashing wings and stabbing beaks, then back at the little starling hopefully cocking its head.

'All right,' he sighed, 'just a few more.' He strode to the boundary wall and trickled a small heap of barley seeds on the ground. 'But that's it,' he said sternly. 'Leave the other ones to grow.'

Oddo had barely started down the field again, when there was a squawk of indignation. The starling was scolding and flapping its wings as the strange boy from Grimmr's field leaned over the boundary stones, grabbed a handful of seeds and stuffed them into his mouth.

'Trust Grimmr not to give his slave enough to eat,' thought Oddo.

When the boy saw Oddo watching, he straightened, his dark eyes flashing defiantly. His cropped hair stood up in red-brown tufts, like winter heather, and his pale face was dotted with tiny brown specks, like the seeds scattered on the ground.

Oddo took a step towards him and held out the basket.

The thrall screwed up his face and shot a stream of chewed-up seeds in Oddo's direction.

'Viking!' he spat. 'Tothaim cen éirge foirib uili!'

Oddo reeled back.

'I . . .'

He shut his mouth quickly as the boy snatched up a lump of dung and weighed it menacingly in his hand. Warily, Oddo turned on his heel. He waited for that clod of dung to hit him in the middle of his back as he reached into his basket and drew out a fistful of seed. He scattered it, moving stiffly, conscious of those eyes burning into him. But when he reached the end of the field and looked round, the thrall had gone back to work.

Oddo puffed his cheeks and let out a breath.

'Rodent!' he muttered. 'That's the last time I try to make friends with him.'

ᛏᛚ ᚲᚨᚱᛒ ᚨ ᚱᛚᚾ

3
The Sheriff's return

In the wood, new shoots of bracken and nettle were poking through the dead leaves of last autumn.

'I'll pick those sprigs for supper on the way home,' thought Thora, as she hurried in the direction of Bolverk's farm.

She reached the edge of the trees, and paused.

To her left, lambs chased each other up and down the mountainside, while ewes enjoyed the fresh spring grass. To her right there were glints of sunlight on water. It was the river, wending its way to fjord and sea – the river that always seemed to carry her off to adventure with her friend Oddo.

In front of her, the rich soil of Bolverk's field was black and gleaming, with rain pelting down on it from a single cloud in the blue sky.

'Oddo's doing,' she thought.

And there he was, standing by the field and talking to the cloud.

'Hey, Oddo!' she called. 'Can you make that rain stop for a moment? I want to show you something.' The downpour petered out, and she raced across the field. 'Look, I've got a new rune for you!'

She crouched down and began to scratch a mark into the damp earth with her finger.

'No!' Oddo pushed her arm away, and scuffed out the line with his toe. 'I'm not trying anything with runes again,' he said. 'You know what happened last time.'

'But this time I've got it right!' she assured him. 'Maybe I can't do spells like the rest of my family, but I *can* copy a rune. Farmer Ulf asked Father to make a ceremony to help his seeds grow well, and Father drew a rune in the earth. I watched so I could show you.'

Stubbornly, Oddo shook his head.

'Your father is Runolf the Rune-maker,' he said. 'If he wants to carve runes to make barley grow, or make someone wise or rich or brave or whatever, that's his job. I'm not trying it again. Anyway, *I* don't need a rune to make seeds grow! You know I can change the weather, and keep pests away just by talking to them. I can grow the best crop in the district. Father said so.'

'Bolverk said that?'

Oddo grinned, and she saw a proud flush of pink steal up his cheeks.

'And he sounded really pleased with me,' he said.

Thora stared at him, remembering the timid boy she'd met two years before, the boy who thought his father didn't love him, who was scared to open his mouth for fear he'd do magic by mistake. Now he was boasting about his powers. For an instant she felt a twinge of regret. He didn't need help from her any more.

She stood up and looked at the wet earth clinging to her apron dress. She gave it a shake.

'You're right, you don't need a rune,' she said. 'But . . . make sure you grow lots of barley, so you've got some to pay the King's taxes when the Sheriff comes back.'

'The Sheriff? Who said he's coming back?'

'Mother. She scried it in the fortune-telling bowl.'

'That's not fair! We already paid.'

'I know, but I guess King Harald's used up all the grain and butter and stuff we sent him last year.'

'How are *you* going to pay?' asked Oddo.

Thora grinned at the sight of his worried face. Oddo knew how difficult it had been for her last time. Thora's family didn't sow seeds or churn butter. They didn't even own a cow. They were spellworkers. Since Thora was the only practical one, they expected her to find a way to pay the taxes. Last year, she'd nearly failed, and her family had come close to losing their home and their freedom. But this time . . .

'Remember that bag of silver I lost?'

'Have you found it?'

'Not yet. But if I go down the river to Gyda's house, I will. I'm sure we dropped it when we climbed out her window.'

'But . . . That was ages ago. Last year. Last time the Sheriff came.'

'Gyda will be keeping it safe for me, if she found it.'

She pictured the midwife's cosy home, and then she saw again the startled look in the old woman's eyes at the sound of Grimmr banging on her door.

'It was funny when I magicked a storm inside her house,' said Oddo. 'And she and Grimmr went screaming around in the dark.'

'And then you tricked them into thinking we'd fallen down the cliff,' said Thora. 'That was mean. Gyda was really worried.'

'Well, what was I supposed to do? I had to stop that greedy Grimmr from chasing us.'

They both swung round to look at Grimmr's farm.

Thora saw a strange boy working in his field.

'Who's *that*?' asked Thora.

'Grimmr's new thrall,' said Oddo. 'Keep away from him. He's dangerous. And crazy.'

'What do you mean?'

'He ate the raw seeds I put down for the birds.'

'That doesn't make him dangerous,' said Thora. 'He's probably starving. Look how skinny he is. I bet Grimmr doesn't feed him.'

'Well, that's no reason to spit at me when I try to be friendly, or swear in a strange language.'

The thrall seemed to sense they were talking about him. He picked up a clod of dung and hurled it over the wall.

'See?'

Thora shook her head. 'Of course he's cross, poor thing. How would *you* feel if someone captured you and turned you into a slave? And look at his bare legs. He must be freezing!' She fingered the pin on her cloak.

'Don't you try giving him your cloak,' warned Oddo. 'He'll just throw something at you.'

ᛊᛏ ᚦᛖ ᚠᛁᛏᛗ,

4
Encounter in the wood

It was a few days later when Thora noticed the funny smell. She was passing the ring of brambles where she'd made her secret garden two summers before. She stopped and sniffed the air. She thought she knew the scent of every plant in the wood, but she didn't recognise this sweet, sickly odour. She eyed the brambles in puzzlement, then caught her breath. There was a hole near the ground – her old secret tunnel gaping open. Someone had cut back the new growth covering the entrance. Some strange person had found the way into the space behind the brambles.

For an instant, Thora thought of her clean apron dress and kirtle, then she dropped to her knees and pushed herself into the hole. She'd grown a lot since last time. The thorny branches overhead caught her hair, and scraped along her back. She pressed herself close against the earth, wriggled forward, and burst into the clearing.

The boy from Grimmr's field was crouched inside, staring at her. She saw the glint of a dagger in his hand and something huge and hairy sprawled across his lap. At his feet was a pit filled with brown, foaming liquid, and out of it rose sweet, sickly fumes.

Thora froze, holding her breath. Then she realised the hairy thing in the boy's arms was just a hide from an ox, and he was using his dagger to scrape off the hairs.

He was the first to break the silence.

'No-m léic m'óenur!' he snarled.

Thora looked at his shaking hands. She saw the bruises and scars on his bare legs, the hollows in his cheeks and the scared look in his eyes.

'I'm your friend,' she whispered, wondering what putrid thing was festering in that brown ooze, making the dreadful stink. 'I'm Thora.' She tapped her chest, and tried to smile as she pointed at him. 'Who are you?'

There was a moment's silence.

'Dúngal,' he answered at last. 'Dúngal mac Flainn.'

Slowly, Thora lifted her hands and unpinned her cloak. She slid it from her shoulders.

'Here, you must be cold.'

Leaning over the pit, she held it towards him.

The boy was silent, watching her warily. Then his hand flashed out and grabbed the cloak. Caught unawares, Thora held on an instant too long. She was yanked off balance, and with a scream, she toppled into the pit.

Brown ooze leapt over her face. Her wet kirtle wrapped around her legs, dragging her down, and for one horrible moment she sank below the surface. Then she stood up, gasping and choking, waist-deep in the dreadful brew. Soft, pulpy objects wobbled under her feet, and something slimy hung over her cheek. As she flicked her head, it fell off, plopping back in the water.

'Auuugh!' she shuddered, but Dúngal was already gripping her arms and hauling her out. She struggled up the slippery wall of the pit, and collapsed onto dry ground. Grinning, Dúngal picked up the cloak and wrapped it around her shoulders.

'Uch, now . . . you cold!' he said.

When he smiled, he looked completely different. His little berry nose turned upwards and his eyes twinkled. Thora tried to smile back. Then Dúngal scooped a slimy object from the pit and squeezed out the water. A lump of oak bark lay in his hand. *Oak bark?*

Dúngal held up the ox hide.

'I . . . make . . .' He pointed at his belt. 'Leather.'

Thora glanced back at the pit, still puzzled.

'Yes.' Dúngal mimed dropping the ox hide into the smelly water. 'Leave many nights in water and . . . bark. Make good leather.'

'But . . . what are you going to do with the leather?'

For a moment, the fierce look was back on Dúngal's face.

Then he bent forward and raised an eyebrow. 'You my . . . friend?' he asked. 'True?'

Thora nodded solemnly.

Dúngal studied her, not speaking. Thora began to shiver with cold. She clenched her teeth hard, to stop them chattering and kept her eyes fixed on his face.

At last he spoke. His voice was hoarse.

'I make curach,' he said.

'Cu . . . *what*?'

'Curach.' He waggled his arms, as if using oars.

'A boat?'

Dúngal nodded eagerly. 'Yes! Curach – boat!'

'But how do you make a boat out of leather?'

Dúngal grinned. 'I know how. At home, all boats leather.'

Thora stared at him. 'What are you going to do with a boat?'

Dúngal wasn't grinning now. He leaned so close, his breath tickled her face.

'Go home,' he whispered.

Thora eyed him anxiously.

'You're going to run away? Escape?'

Dúngal nodded.

'But where do you have to get to? Where's your home?'

His voice cracked as he spoke the one word, 'Ériu,' and Thora saw his eyes glisten with tears.

'Ériu? Where's that?'

'You call . . . Ireland.'

'*Ireland?* But that's a long way. That's where the Viking raiders go . . .' Her voice trailed away as Dúngal's eyes blazed with anger.

'Vikings!' He spat viciously.

Thora bit her lip, but she had to go on.

'Dúngal, the Viking raiders have great big longships and teams of men to sail them. You can't get to . . . to Ériu in a little boat made from leather. You'll capsize. You'll drown! You'll never make it!'

Dúngal glared. 'Drowning better than being thrall!'

ᛁᛏ ᛁᛋ ᚠ ᚱᚢᚾᚦ

5

A fine curach

The horse whinnied softly, and Dúngal opened one eye. Over the low barn door he could see the first hint of dawn. He lay another minute, snuggled in the straw. Then he groaned, and clambered to his feet.

Outside, the cold air stung his eyes, and his numb feet stumbled on the freezing cobbles of the yard. He pushed aside the door hangings and slipped into the house. As usual, Grimmr lay on his back, snoring. Dúngal remembered the first time he'd seen this fat pig. Grimmr had been glaring round the slave market with his bulging eyes, searching for the smallest and cheapest thrall. Dúngal lifted his hand and rubbed under his chin. He would never free himself of the memory of the iron fetter round his neck, the way it had jerked up and hit him on the chin whenever the taller slaves beside him had moved.

The warmth of the room was making his nose run. He sniffed as he crouched by the firepit in the middle of the room and blew on the embers. He picked up more kindling to feed the fire, and cursed as a thorn stabbed his finger. He broke off the spike, then a slow smile stole over his face. Creeping across the room, he dropped the thorn into Grimmr's shoe. Just at that moment, the man snorted and stretched. Dúngal scuttled back to the hearth.

'Wood nearly gone. Cut more?' Dúngal nodded at the woodpile and waited tensely for Grimmr's answer. Fetching firewood would give him an excuse to go to the woods with the axe. He could cut the branches he needed for his boat.

'Why are we always running out of wood?' Grimmr grumbled. 'You must be wasting it, you lazy slug.' Dúngal held his breath. 'But, yes, go and cut some more − after you've made my breakfast.'

He swung his legs out of bed and Dúngal watched eagerly as he pulled on his shoes and stood up.

'Auuggh!'

Hopping wildly, Grimmr kicked off the offending shoe and hobbled to the table.

Dúngal struggled to keep a solemn face as he served his master steaming porridge. But his glee vanished the moment he tasted his own breakfast. The lump of stale

28

bread was made from spiky husks of barley, and it was so dry it stuck in his throat. As he leaned over the fire to cook fresh cakes for Grimmr, the delicious smell of frying butter made his belly snarl with longing. He slammed the hot griddle on the table, and turned for the door. The water bucket stood in front of him. Furtively, he gave it a shove, sending it toppling towards the fire. Water spilt over the flames, and smoke poured upwards.

'You clumsy fool!' Grimmr stumbled away from the table, coughing and flapping his arms.

Grinning, Dúngal tugged the axe from its hook.

'I fetch more wood,' he said.

Grimmr's shoe was lying on the floor where he'd kicked it. Hidden by the cloud of smoke, Dúngal thrust it out of sight behind a wooden chest.

'Try to find that, you big bully,' he muttered. Then he scurried out of the room.

For the next few months, whenever he could, Dúngal found an excuse to go to the wood. He hunted, or picked wild berries, or chopped wood, then slipped into his secret place to work on his boat.

Sometimes the girl Thora would visit him while he worked. He would hear a scuffling in the tunnel, and look up, his hand reaching for the axe. Then her smiling face would pop up from the hole, rosy cheeks grimy with soil, her hair tousled.

She brought him strange food to eat: tiny birds' eggs boiled in their shells, leaves she picked in the wood, even smelly seaweed.

'At home, that's what I spread on the fields, for fertiliser,' he thought, but he managed to swallow it.

Thora cut the rawhide strips that would hold his curach together, while he whittled and shaped ash branches for the frame. At last it was time to fit the first small hoop into place. Thora handed him a rawhide strip and he bound it tight. He grinned proudly and picked up the next hoop, but when he tried to tie it down, it sprang out of his hands. Again and again he grabbed it, but it wriggled as if it was live. Tears of frustration pricked his eyes. He was about to give up and hurl the piece of wood across the clearing when he saw Thora's eyes, bright with anticipation. Cursing, he wrestled it into place, and wiped his sweaty face with his sleeve. Then he picked up the next hoop.

Slowly, the skeleton of the boat began to take shape.

Thora chatted while they worked, only stopping when there were footsteps or voices beyond the brambles. Then they would both freeze, waiting till the sounds faded. Once they heard a girl with a strident voice telling someone else what to do.

'That's Astrid,' whispered Thora. 'My bossy older sister.'

'Have you got sisters?' she asked later.

'Dias . . . two. Little ones,' mumbled Dúngal.

He was embarrassed to speak, fumbling to find the right words in this strange tongue. But Thora kept asking him questions.

'Tell me about your family,' she said.

Gradually, as the weeks passed, Dúngal found the Viking words flowing more easily to his lips.

'What do your sisters wear?' asked Thora. 'Do they weave their own clothes, like this?'

'Weave, yes, but not like this.' He pinched the rough woollen cloth. 'Not from wool. They use leaves – special, long leaves.'

'I can make rope out of leaves,' said Thora. 'Nettle leaves! Hey, will you need ropes for your boat? Are you going to have a sail? I could make them for you.'

One day, Dúngal picked up three rawhide strips, plaited flowers into them and wound them round Thora's long, honey-coloured hair.

'Pretty,' he said. 'Like my . . . sethir. My sisters. Also, they wear . . .' He pointed to the brooches on her apron dress. 'Like this, in their ears.'

'Pins? In their ears?!' squealed Thora.

'Not pins, gold.'

'My brooches aren't gold,' said Thora. 'I think they're bronze. Do your sisters wear brooches? And necklaces, and bangles?'

'Yes. Much gold in Ériu.'

'What are your sisters' names?'

'Aífe and Eithne.'

Dúngal picked up a stick and scraped their names in the damp earth near the pit.

When he looked up again, Thora was gaping at him.

'You can do runes,' she breathed. 'You're magic!'

'Magic?' He looked down at the writing. 'No. These are just words, my sisters' names.'

'You can . . . *draw* . . . people's names?'

'Of course. Can't you?'

Thora shook her head. 'Does everyone in Ireland draw names? Where do you learn?'

'From the priests. They are very clever. They can draw many, many words, not just names. I go to the priest. Other boys go. And we learn to draw words.'

'Can you do my name?'

Dúngal thought for a moment, then scraped her name into the soil.

'And that says Thora?'

'Yes.'

'So you don't have magic in Ériu?'

'Of course we do. We have the Sídaigi . . . magic people. They are tiny, but very . . . powerful. On the nights of the big fires, when the farmers plant or harvest – that is when we see them. We must give them food and drink to make them happy. If not, they do bad things.'

'Just like here!' said Thora.

'You have Sídaigi too?'

'We call them Little Folk. And when it's a festival,

we give them presents to make them happy, like you do. Tell more about Ériu. What's your house like?'

So Dúngal described the ringfort where his family and all his kinsfolk lived, and the big, open-air cooking fire where they gathered in the evenings to eat, and tell stories, and listen to Grandfather sing.

'When I go back and sit at the fire again, Grandfather will make a song about my adventures.'

He told about the summer meadows outside the walls, where bees droned and sheep stood knee-deep in buttercups. He described the brook where the mustard-flavoured watercress grew. And, best of all, he described the round house with its high, pointy roof, so different from the squat, turf-covered houses of Norway. As he spoke, he pictured his father stooping to come through the low door, laughing at Aífe and Eithne romping round the floor with a litter of kittens. He could see his mother lighting the beeswax candles, filling the room with their sweet scent.

'Máthair,' he whispered.

And then he thought of the smelly, smoky oil lamps in Grimmr's house, his lonely nights sleeping in the barn with the animals . . .

He jumped as Thora's voice broke in and she thrust the axe into his hand. 'Don't mope. You're making this fine curach. You'll get back to your family. I know you will.'

ᛏᛚ ᚺᛗᚱᛚ

6

A basket full of holes

'Oddo, we've got to help him!' pleaded Thora. 'He's building a boat and he wants to go back to Ireland.'

'So? I'm not stopping him! I'll be very pleased, thank you, when I can go outside again and not have an idiot throw dung at me.'

'He only did it that one time.'

'Oh, so that makes it all right, does it?'

'Don't be silly. If you'd just been kidnapped, you wouldn't be too friendly either.'

'Well, fine with me. I don't want to be friends. I won't be stupid enough to go near him again. And I don't see why you want to shove yourself under his nose every five seconds. Have you *looked* at him? He's

34

got speckles all over his face, and silly short hair that sticks up like barley stubble, and . . .'

'Don't be mean. It's not Dúngal's fault someone turned him into a slave and chopped his hair off.'

At the sound of her agitated voice, Hairydog, who'd been dozing in a patch of sunshine, woke up and began to yip excitedly. Oddo scuffed the ground.

'Well, there's nothing I can do about it,' he growled.

He glanced up again. Thora's eyes were sparkling.

'Yes there is. I've got it all planned. We'll both go with him in the curach – that's what he calls his boat – and you can use your magic powers to make the wind blow the right way till we get to Ireland. If a storm comes, you can stop it. We'll get there in no time.'

'What?! You expect me to spend days on end stuck on a boat with that lemming?'

'Of course. You'll like Dúngal when you get to know him. Come on, I'll show you where he's building the boat.' She pulled on his sleeve excitedly. 'Dúngal's—'

'Dúngal's a stupid name. Sounds like you're swallowing something. Dúngal. Dúngal.'

'Come and look. He's started making the boat. He's building the frame out of ash branches and then he's going to cover it with ox hides. I'm going to weave the sail, and make the ropes out of nettles, the way Hallveig and Erp showed me at the Gula Thing.'

They were in the wood now and Thora came to a halt in front of the bramble patch.

'It's in here,' she whispered. 'Where I used to have my secret garden.'

'Peuugh, what's the stink?'

'The tanning pit, where Dúngal's curing the hides. Come on.'

A moment later, Oddo wriggled out of the tunnel, and found himself face-to-face with Dúngal. The Irish boy looked as startled as Oddo. He scrambled to his feet, scowling and waving his axe.

'Viking!'

This time, Oddo was wearing his dagger. He whipped it out of his belt and glared back. This time, he wasn't going to be intimidated by a thrall.

'Oh, stop it, you two. Dúngal, put the axe down. Oddo's a friend.'

Hairydog's head popped out of the tunnel. At the sight of Dúngal, the bristles rose on her neck. Thora reached over to grab her as she bared her teeth and let out a growl.

Oddo kept the dagger in his hand till Dúngal lowered his axe.

'Come on, silly,' said Thora, 'come and look at the boat. It's so clever the way Dúngal's made it.'

She edged round the pit, Hairydog at her heels. Oddo followed, gagging ostentatiously and holding his nose.

When he reached the other side, he eyed the boat.

'What's so great about this?' He was still holding his nose. 'Looks like a basket full of holes.'

He glanced sideways at Dúngal, then prodded the frame with his foot. It trembled and one of the loose stringers rattled to the ground. Oddo saw the thrall clench his fists. Thora, shooting a furious glance at him, picked up the piece of ash, and tried to fit it to the boat.

'Is this the right place?' she asked.

'A díbergaig brénanalaig!' Dúngal snarled at Oddo. Scowling, he tied the stringer into place while Thora held it steady.

'You really plan to sail to Ireland in *this*?' demanded Oddo. The curach was tiny, smaller than *The Cormorant* that his father rowed to market. 'You won't fit three people in there.'

'Yes we will,' said Thora.

But Dúngal looked up, his eyes wide. 'Three?' He pointed at Oddo. 'You'll not be coming!'

'Suit yourself,' said Oddo. 'I didn't want to come anyway. That thing's going to sink the minute it hits the water. Thora, you can't be serious about going in it. Come on, Hairydog, let's get out of here.'

'Dúngal,' he could hear Thora pleading as he turned away, 'you don't understand. We need Oddo. He's magic. He can make the boat go where we want.'

Wriggling into the tunnel, he listened for Dúngal's answer. 'Upp, I'm not needing magic,' said the thrall stubbornly. 'That's a good boat I've made.'

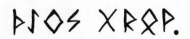

7
Around the firepit

'What are you going to tell your parents?' asked Oddo. '*They* won't want you to sail to Ireland in that silly curach.'

Thora shrugged. 'It wouldn't worry them. They know I can look after myself. But I don't think I'll tell them, anyway. I'll just say I'm going to Gyda's to fetch the silver.' Oddo was silent. 'It's not a lie. I will go to Gyda's — on the way back.'

'Not if the boat sinks, and you're drowned.'

'It won't sink. Dúngal's going to cover the leather with fat to make it waterproof.'

'And where does he think he's going to get all the fat from?'

'*I'll* get it. I'll go round and ask all the farmers to save me their fat next time they kill a sheep. I'll pretend I need it for my potions.'

Oddo shook his head. 'You're mad, risking your life for that poophead.'

But the next time Bolverk slaughtered a sheep, Oddo filled a bucket with blood-streaked lumps of yellowy fat and carried it through the wood to the house-over-the-hill. He found Thora in a cleared patch among the weeds, tending her herb garden.

'Look how everything's growing,' she called excitedly. She showed him the little pea plants with their tiny curling shoots, the buds of baby cabbages, the scented rosemarin. 'I could do with a bit of rain, though.'

Then she noticed the bucket in his hand. 'Oh! Is that for the boat? I can boil it right now.'

'Can't let you both drown,' growled Oddo.

The sound of raindrops followed them into the house.

Inside, the room was thick with smoke. Oddo picked his way across a floor covered with mysterious lumps. He trod on something by mistake, and it squelched unpleasantly under his foot. Screeching figures leapt out of the gloom. Oddo dodged as Granny Hulda, followed by Astrid and Edith, danced round him, tossing objects in the air and singing a strange chant. Something landed on Oddo's head and bounced onto the floor. It was a dead bird. Thora swooped on it eagerly.

'That'll do for supper,' she said happily.

Oddo felt a sticky cobweb trail across his face; and the herbs hanging from the rafters sprinkled dusty, scented leaves on his hair.

They reached the firepit where little Ketil was rolling a lump of dough on the floor.

'Cook it now!' he said, holding it up. It was grey and covered with lumps of grit and feathers.

Thora's mother, Finnhilda, took it from him. But instead of setting it to cook on a griddle, she thrust her bare hand into the flames, and held it there, muttering a spell.

Granny Hulda stopped prancing, and hovered, her beady eyes roving around the room, her thin fingers plucking the air. She looked like a small, curled-up beetle.

'Is that the farmer's boy,' she asked, 'the one who thinks he can do spellwork?'

A lanky boy shot up in front of Oddo. 'What runes do you know?' Erik demanded.

'I . . . can't do runes,' said Oddo.

'Huh.' Erik tossed a stone that almost hit Oddo in the face.

'Can you turn invisible? I can turn invisible.' Ketil leapt up from the floor and ran to fetch his goatskin cloak.

'What about flower spells? Can you do this?' asked Edith. 'Show him, Sissa.' A tiny girl with wide eyes and wispy hair picked up a log from the woodpile. A moment later, leaves and flowers sprouted all over it. The child chuckled, and Oddo shook his head.

'He can't do anything,' sneered Astrid. 'It's just Thora's boasting.'

'He can too!' Oddo was startled by the fury in Thora's voice. '*Show* them, Oddo.'

Embarrassed, Oddo glanced at the chimney hole. Everyone was watching. He was about to call for a spot of rain, when a siskin darted across the space with a flutter of yellow feathers.

'Hey,' he called. 'Come here.'

The little bird turned in mid-flight, dived through the hole and alighted on his outstretched hand.

'That's not hard,' said Astrid.

Oddo bent his mouth close to the feathered head, and whispered.

The next moment, the siskin swooped across the room, and grasped a strand of Astrid's hair in its tiny beak.

'Ow!' squealed Astrid, and tried to pull free. But the bird kept tugging as if it was pulling on a juicy worm. 'Ow! Make it let go!'

'What a pity,' said Oddo. 'I'm not very good at spell-work. I don't know how to make it stop.'

He winked at Thora. Hastily she bent her head and tipped the lumps of fat into a cauldron.

While Astrid ran around the room squealing and

holding her head, Thora added water and hung the pot on the fire. Her other brothers and sisters chased after Astrid, shouting instructions. Oddo caught the siskin's eye. It let go and flew away.

Astrid came to a halt, panting, her face scarlet. 'You . . . You . . .'

'You asked for it, Astrid,' chortled Harald, and skipped out of the way as she spun towards him.

The fat in the cauldron began to bubble. Shrivelled grey cracklings and bits of blood and foam rose to the surface. 'Like boats in a sea,' said Harald, peering over the edge.

Oddo stared at the crispy curls swirling among the bubbles.

'Bet they float better than Dúngal's curach,' he muttered. He glanced at Thora.

She ignored him, and used a wooden ladle to skim the surface. Harald snatched a piece of crackling and popped it in his mouth. Oddo stared as his teeth crunched it into flakes, and imagined a tiny boat, disintegrating . . .

'Thora, you're not really planning to go off in that joke of a boat, are you?' he demanded.

Thora pursed her lips, sat down and began to pluck the feathers off the dead bird.

'Stir the pot for me, will you?' she said.

A whirlwind of floating feathers was added to the fumes of smoke and boiling fat.

Oddo stared at his friend, and imagined her trying to sail all the way to Ireland in the curach. With only that blockhead for company.

At last, Thora covered the opening of an empty keg with a piece of weaving, and asked Oddo to hold it while she tilted the cauldron. He turned his face away as the liquid fat poured out in a stinking, steaming stream – through the cloth and into the keg.

'Now, I'll leave that in the storehouse to cool,' said Thora. 'Tomorrow there'll be a clean layer of white fat sitting on the top, and that's what Dúngal will use on his leather.'

On the way home, clothes and hair reeking of fat, Oddo passed the bramble patch where Dúngal was building his boat. He halted, and looked around. There was nobody in sight, and no sound coming from the brambles. Furtively, he slid into the tunnel.

On the other side, he scrambled to his feet and gazed at the curach. It was even smaller than he'd remembered. Compared to a wooden Viking ship, it looked as fragile as the skeleton of a bird. Could it really cross the sea to another land?

ᛁᛏ ᛁᛚᚲᛋ ᛚᛁᚲ ᚦᛁᛋ...

8
Oddo's dilemma

'Oddo, the milk's going everywhere!'

Oddo started guiltily. Milk was foaming over the edges of the vat onto the earth floor of the dairy.

'What on earth were you thinking?' said his mother.

Oddo didn't answer. When he'd tilted the bucket, it hadn't been milk he saw pouring downwards, but the sea swamping a little boat. These days, everything he saw and heard reminded him of waves and storms and flapping sails. He was haunted by visions of a tiny curach tossing in a stormy sea, and an image of Thora clinging to its side and wailing to him, 'Oddo, stop the storm!'

When he left the dairy, he saw the real Thora hurrying across the paddock.

'Hey,' he called, 'I'm over here.'

To his annoyance, she didn't stop.

'Can't talk now,' she flung over her shoulder. 'Taking this to Dúngal.' She waggled a strand of fresh green nettle rope.

The boy on the other side of the fence straightened from his hoeing and waved. Oddo watched, fuming, as Thora joined him.

'You've always got time to talk to *Dúngal*,' he muttered.

He turned his back and stomped towards the river, but as he dipped his bucket in the water, he saw the little boat again. This time it was filling slowly with seawater and Thora, instead of wailing for him, was clinging to Dúngal. Angrily, he thrust the bucket deep. He let go and watched it sink down, the ripples closing over it. Then he grabbed the handle and hauled it out. He slammed it so hard on the bank, water sloshed all over his breeches.

'Barley's come up beautifully again,' said Bolverk at supper. 'You're turning into a real farmer.'

Oddo knew those words should make him glow with pride, but he just stared down at his plate, prodding the crumbs with his finger.

'Could the crop manage without rain for a couple of days?' he asked. 'If I . . . go away for a bit?'

'Away? Where?'

'I . . .' Oddo frowned. He'd worked so hard to earn his father's trust and respect. What would happen if he found out Oddo was planning to help a slave escape, and sail to Ireland in a boat made of twigs and bits of animal skin?

'Thora asked me to go with her to Gyda's,' he mumbled. 'Down the river.'

'I haven't seen Thora for weeks,' said Sigrid. 'She must be very busy.'

'Huh,' grunted Oddo.

'Such a sweet girl. Remember that summer you were sick, Husband, and she helped me? Just like a daughter.'

'Well,' Bolverk brushed the crumbs from his beard, 'you'd have to walk there. I need *The Cormorant* for fishing.'

'But . . . would the seedlings be all right?'

'Of course, of course. Just give them a good soaking before you leave.'

'It's a long way to Gyda's,' said Sigrid anxiously.

Bolverk slapped the table.

'Have you forgotten, woman, that your son walked all the way home from the Gula Thing? He can manage an easy stroll to Gyda's and back.'

Oddo gulped.

'I wish it *was* just that,' he thought.

The next day, he waylaid Thora as she struggled through the wood with a heavy bundle.

'What's that?' He pointed at the heap of woollen cloth.

'Nothing to interest you. It's the sail for the curach.' Thora stuck out her chin. 'We're leaving tomorrow.'

There was a silence. Oddo took a deep breath. 'Well, what do you want me to bring?'

Thora stared. Then she dropped the bundle and flung her arms around him. Oddo felt as if a weight that had been pressing on him for days was suddenly lifted. He hugged her back, and breathed the smell of her sun-warmed hair against his cheek.

That night, Oddo was too excited to swallow his supper.

'Remember to wake me before it's light,' he told his mother. 'We want to start really early.'

'Off to bed now, then,' said Sigrid.

But when Oddo lay on the sleeping bench, he felt as if someone had poked a stick in his belly and was churning it round and round. In the glow of the dying fire, he gazed around the room; at the twig broom leaning in a corner, the pots neatly stacked on the shelves, the wisps of smoke curling from the snuffed oil lamps, the tall shape of his mother's loom and the clay weights on the threads clinking softly.

'If that boat sinks, I'll never see these again,' he thought.

When Sigrid shook his shoulder, it seemed as if he hadn't slept at all. He watched her ladling out his porridge and tried to fix the picture in his mind: Bolverk, a dark, sleeping shape in the background, his snores reverberating through the room, and Sigrid, her round pink cheeks glowing in the firelight.

He sat at the table to eat, but he couldn't stop shivering, and he had to force the porridge down his throat. When Sigrid pinned the cloak around his shoulders, he reached out to give her a clumsy hug. As he passed the bed, he touched his father's hair gently with the tips of his fingers.

Outside, Hairydog bounded ahead, yapping with excitement. It was barely light when Oddo wriggled through the tunnel, but Dúngal and Thora were there already. As soon as he appeared, they leapt to their feet. Thora grabbed the oars.

'Right, let's go. Hurry!'

Oddo and Dúngal picked up the boat, and as Oddo felt the lightness of it in his hand, his heart plummeted. They could never cross an ocean in this.

They turned towards the tunnel.

'Uh, how are we going to get it out?' asked Oddo.

They all stared at the opening, too narrow even for this tiny boat to fit through. Oddo felt a wave of relief. 'We won't be able to go!' he thought. But then he saw the disappointment on the others' faces.

'Make the hole bigger!' cried Dúngal. He dropped his end of the boat and began tearing at the thorny brambles with his bare hands. 'Help me!'

'Wait, I'll get an axe!' said Oddo resignedly. 'Hairydog, you dig the ground.'

Hairydog's paws churned up the soil as Oddo raced for home.

Back again, the axe in his hand, he yelled at the others to stand back. He slashed at the dense, spiky wall of trees and bushes. Thorny twigs and leaves flew around him, scratching his face and catching in his hair.

'Try now,' he gasped.

He doubled over, trying to catch his breath, as the little curach slid through the gap. He saw Thora glance at the axe in his hand, then into his face. Why was she looking so worried? And then it hit him. Like a punch in the belly. Thora had warned him how to chop a tree. She'd told him to ask the tree's forgiveness first, because of his magic powers. If he didn't . . . Something awful would happen to him. He dropped the axe to the ground, and wiped his hands nervously on his tunic. But it was too late now.

With a feeling of doom, he hoisted up his end of the boat and followed Dúngal down to the river.

9
Which way?

'Hurry!' Dúngal urged. 'It's late. Grimmr will wake and see I'm gone. Uch!' He stumbled over a tree root and the curach slipped from his grasp. He clutched his tunic in exasperation, then bent to lift the boat again. 'Wait. Turn it over. Lift it over your head.'

'How'm I supposed to see where I'm going?' Oddo's voice echoed inside the hollow body of the boat.

'Look down.'

Dúngal watched his feet flash over the ground. In a moment, he glimpsed the water.

'Stop, we're there.'

As he lowered the boat, he heard shouts and running footsteps. Before he could dive for cover, two figures came crashing through the trees. They were boys, long and lanky like Oddo. The taller one raced in front, holding something above his head, while the younger tried to reach it, calling angrily. The sounds faded as they sped into the wood.

Dúngal sprang into action, flipping the curach the right way up.

'Oddo, do you think they saw you?' he hissed.

'Me?' Oddo looked bewildered.

'They were your brothers, weren't they?'

'No. They were Thora's brothers.'

'Oh. They looked like you.'

'Stop babbling,' said Thora. 'Who cares what they look like? Let's get this boat in the water and get out of here.' She turned and reached into the bush. 'Here's the sail,' she called, her voice muffled. 'Now, where's the mast?'

She crawled backwards, dragging the heap of cloth. Oddo was still on one knee, staring into the wood. Dúngal found the end of the mast.

'Oddo, aren't you going to help?' he snapped. He laid the mast along the bank, and bound the yard to the top of it. 'Here, hold this up.' Oddo staggered to his feet, the long ends of the yard sticking out either side of him.

'I'll tie on the sail,' said Thora.

In a few minutes, they were ready to raise the mast. Thora knelt in the curach to guide the foot into position. Dúngal gripped the forestay and began to haul. His mouth was dry. If the mast didn't fit in the wooden step . . .

'It's in!' yelled Thora as it thudded into place. Dúngal gulped with relief.

But when the long pole was raised, the curach wobbled alarmingly. Oddo grabbed the side to stop it toppling over.

'I told you this was hopeless,' he yelled.

'Just get it in the water!' said Dúngal crossly.

But as he pushed it down the bank, he felt the sour taste of bile in his throat. Maybe Oddo was right. Maybe it wouldn't float.

The curach slid into the river and Dúngal threw himself aboard. The tall mast tilted, the boat heeled, and water slopped over the side.

'It's going to sink!'

Frantically he rolled himself the other way, and as his weight shifted, the boat steadied. He lay on his back, the boat bobbing under him, and stared at the mast, quivering but vertical above his head. He could feel the slap of waves against the leather. Slowly, cautiously, he sat up.

Thora was leaping and cheering on the bank.

'You did it! You're floating!' she squealed.

Grinning, Dúngal picked up an oar. He lowered it over the side of the boat and began to paddle in a circle.

'A óen,' he counted.

He paddled round again.

'A dó.'

'What are you *doing*?' called Thora. 'I thought you were in a hurry!'

'Bringing the blessing of the sun,' said Dúngal. 'Three circles for luck. This is the last one . . . A trí!' He completed the turn, and headed for the bank. 'Watch where you step. Don't tip it again.'

'Careful, Hairydog,' warned Oddo, pulling the eager dog back.

As they clambered in, the curach rocked violently. Oddo's face paled and he sat down abruptly, clutching the sides.

When the cauldron, fur blankets and pots of food were stowed around their feet, Dúngal proudly unfurled the sail. It hung limp, and the boat bobbed in the current.

'Okay, Oddo.' Thora pointed downriver. 'Make the wind blow!'

They all peered up anxiously; even Hairydog raised her muzzle and squinted at the sail. Dúngal felt a breeze ripple through his hair. The woollen cloth of the sail shivered, flapped once, then bellied outwards. The curach bucked and shot away.

'Move to the other side!' shouted Dúngal, grabbing the steering oar.

'We're sailing!' yelled Thora, but Oddo held up a drenched sleeve.

'We're leaking!' he bellowed. He jabbed with his finger. Water was trickling through the holes where the leather was stitched to the frame. 'I said this would happen.'

Thora snatched up the wooden dipper and prepared to bail.

'Don't worry!' said Dúngal. 'When the leather gets wet, the holes'll close up.' But as they neared the river mouth and the open sea, he saw the high, thrashing surf. His hand clenched on the steering oar. Would his little boat stand up against those angry waves? As the first breaker pounded towards them, he seized Thora's arm. 'Hold tight!'

The mountain of water reared over their heads, white foam dripping from its crest. But the curach rose too, dancing and bobbing on the swell. The wave slid beneath her hull, then faded away, just a harmless ripple. The curach floated like a gull, rising and plunging with the sea.

Dúngal felt as if his whole body was melting with relief, and there were tears running down his cheeks.

Thora laughed in delight. 'Oddo, didn't I tell you Dúngal could build a real boat?'

With spray in their eyes, and salt on their lips, Thora and Dúngal hooted at the waves. Hairydog, teetering on her hind legs, barked at the seabirds wheeling overhead and the long-necked gannets, diving for fish. Graceful little terns jinked and squawked between the wave crests, chased by a greedy skua trying to snatch the catch from their bright red beaks.

On the yardarm, a tie worked free and whipped loudly in the wind.

'I'd better fix it,' said Dúngal.

'Shall I lower the yard?'

'No! Don't slow the boat. I can reach.'

'Rubbish,' said Oddo. 'You're not tall enough. I'll do it.'

'I can fix it,' said Dúngal. 'You wouldn't know what to do.'

He stacked the fur blankets, then rested the big iron cauldron upside-down on top of them for a step. When he climbed up, it wobbled. He had to grab the mast to steady himself before he could lift his arms to tighten the strap.

'Careful!' warned Thora.

He grinned and looked down.

'Déccaid! Watch!' Choosing the right moment, he leaned away from the mast, and balanced. 'How's that?' he cried, stretching out his arms and rocking.

The sail slackened and gave a noisy flap. Dúngal glanced round in surprise.

'Where's the wind?' he demanded.

'You didn't tell me which way to go,' said Oddo. 'I can't read your mind.'

Dúngal glared at him.

'First, to the Isles of Faer,' he said.

'West, then,' said Thora.

There was a *whoosh* and the boat heeled over. Caught

unawares, Dúngal swayed over the waves, his arms whirling. He heard Thora's yelp of alarm, then he toppled backwards into the pit of the curach. As he fell, he saw the grin on Oddo's face.

'I told you to let me do it.'

Dúngal sat up, scowling, and rubbed his elbow. Now the curach was flying over the waves. He leaned against the side and squinted through the spray.

'Where to after the Isles?' said Thora.

'South. I think.'

'You *think*!' Oddo's squawk was like an angry seabird. 'What do you mean you *think*?! You've got us hurtling around in this eggshell in the middle of the sea, and you don't even know where we're going?!'

'You didn't have to come. I could have found it by myself.'

At that moment, water sloshed over the side of the boat. Oddo seized the dipper and began to bail furiously.

'I said you were a lemming. Only a lemming would be stupid enough to drop into the sea and drown itself on purpose.'

'Upp! Stupid yourself,' Dúngal retorted. 'What about your spells? If you're so clever, why don't you use your magic to find the way?'

Dúngal thought Oddo was going to hurl the dipperful of water in his face.

'Dúngal, don't be silly,' said Thora.

'*Me* silly?'

'Magic can't do everything. Oddo can't . . .'

'Oh, can't I?' demanded Oddo. 'I can do a better job than that fluffhead.' He flung the dipper into the bottom of the boat. 'I'll do a shape-change and go look for his stupid Ériu.'

'But . . .' Thora was looking flustered. 'Did you bring a wand? What about the magic circle?'

'I can manage without one.'

'But Oddo, it won't be safe . . .'

'Pig's poop. You fuss too much. I did it once before and it was fine.' He ripped open his pouch and pulled out the fire-lighting tools. 'I can do it with a real fire . . . I just need something to burn.' He pounced on a length of nettle rope and began to saw it with his dagger. 'This'll do.'

'That's our spare rope,' protested Dúngal. 'What if the other ones break?' He eyed the lines flexing and twanging with the billowing sail.

'They won't break.' Oddo was gritting his teeth as he hacked at the rope. 'Thora made them. They're tough.' He grabbed the cauldron. 'I'll light the fire in here.'

'No!' Thora took hold of the other side and tugged.

'What's happening?' demanded Dúngal. 'What's a . . . shape-change?'

'Oddo rides in an animal shape while his real body stays behind. But . . . he's supposed to be protected by a magic circle. I wish you hadn't called him stupid. Oddo, you mustn't!'

She tried to drag the cauldron away, but Oddo hung over its edge, striking the steel against the flint. Yellow sparks flew through the air, and a tiny flame flickered among the dry strands of rope. Oddo dropped his fire tools, snatched the cauldron back, and blew on the fire.

'Now, make sure you keep this going,' he puffed, 'or I won't be able to get back from my shape-change!'

'But . . .'

'The wind'll keep west for a couple of days. Just head for the Isles of Faer. I'll meet you there.'

'But . . .' Thora was getting more and more agitated.

'Sshh!' He hunched into a ball, hugging his knees. 'I'm going to ride as a seabird,' he whispered. 'One of those red-beaked terns.'

'But . . .'

Dúngal watched with interest as a glazed look came into Oddo's eyes.

ᚱᛚᛏᛟᛚᚠ

10
Shape-change

As Oddo glared into the depths of the cauldron, the flickering strands glowed brighter. Flames filled the cauldron and shot upwards in a sheet of golden light, and beyond, perched on the side of the curach, was the shape of a bird.

Oddo's body seemed to flow towards the flames. His heartbeat quickened, faster, faster. The blood pounded in his head. The wind was roaring, trying to knock him off the boat. He hunched down, and clutched the wood tighter with his feet.

Hairydog barked and launched herself towards him. Instinctively, Oddo raised his arms and pushed downwards. With a shock, he felt his body lifting. The solid wood under his feet fell away and he surged forward.

The wind was lifting him, carrying him. He was flying! In a moment he was far from the boat, far out over the sea.

He flicked his wings and bounded, like an arrow springing off a bow. He sped across the water, the wind rushing through his feathers.

'I can fly!' he thought, exultantly.

He rolled his wings through the air, like oars sweeping through water. Higher, he soared, higher and faster. He watched the waves streaming past. From up in the sky, they looked like harmless ripples.

'How do I turn?' he wondered. 'Maybe that's like rowing, too.' He beat one wing faster than the other, and managed to veer round in a curve.

The curach came into sight, the figures inside it all scanning the sky. But only Hairydog could see his magical bird shape. As Oddo drew closer, she yipped a welcome, while Dúngal and Thora looked blankly upwards, even when he swooped right over their heads.

'Kik kik kik!' he called. But of course they couldn't hear him.

He stretched his wings and began to drift, buoyed on air. He could feel the currents lifting him, carrying him, like a boat on a gentle sea. He skimmed the waves, then hovered for a moment, watching the silver backs of the darting fish. Suddenly his wings snapped against his sides and he was plunging like a stone. He hit the water with a splash, his beak stabbed, then he was in the air again, water droplets showering him in rainbow-coloured sparkles and a live fish wriggling down his throat.

In the same instant he heard the whirr of some-thing diving through the air. He glanced up and saw a huge skua swooping towards him. Oddo tried to twist out of the way, but his pursuer twisted with him. The vicious talons slashed at his wings, then gripped hold of his tail feathers and dragged him backwards. He squawked in fright, and the skua grabbed its chance to rip the fish from Oddo's gaping beak and sweep away with it.

Frightened and dishevelled, Oddo wobbled back to the curach. His feet fumbled for a perch on the yardarm, and his wings flopped against his sides. He huddled there, swaying with the rhythm of the boat, his feathers torn and ruffled. As soon as his body stopped quivering, his head twisted towards his back and burrowed under his tail to pick up some preening oil. With the pointy tip of his beak he nibbled his feathers, rubbing them with the oil to make them smooth. He straightened his two long tail feathers, then started on his wings, stroking and rearranging. Only when all his plumes were neat and mended did he peer down at the boat.

The fire was still burning inside the cauldron, and Hairydog was curled around it. Oddo watched Thora cut a piece of cheese and hand it to Dúngal. She leaned towards him, the wind lifting up her long, honey-coloured hair so that it wrapped around his head. They looked cosy and contented, not thinking about him at all. They even had their backs turned on his boy shape at the foot of the mast.

'I've left Thora alone with that oaf,' thought Oddo crossly.

For an instant, he was tempted to abandon his shape-change. The flames in the cauldron reached out invitingly towards him. Then he saw Thora shade her eyes and peer out to sea.

'Can you see any land yet?' she asked.

She was speaking to Dúngal, but Oddo lifted his red webbed feet and twisted round on his perch so he, too, could look. Even with his bird's-eye view, all that was visible in every direction was endless sea.

'If I get back in that boat,' he thought, 'we could sail for ever and ever, and never find Ireland. I'd never get rid of that conceited, puffed-up—'

At that moment, Thora turned to check inside the cauldron. So, she hadn't forgotten him. She picked up a strand of nettle rope to feed the flames, but as she leaned forward, Dúngal tugged her skirt and held up the hunk of cheese.

'Leave her alone, you poophead,' thought Oddo crossly. He lifted his tail and sent a blob of white shooting downwards. It plopped onto the red hair, and trickled across Dúngal's cheek. Oddo squawked with glee. 'Now you're really a poophead!'

A pity Thora couldn't see it. But his droppings were no more visible to her than his magical bird shape.

He rested a moment longer, then, with a last longing glance into the boat, he lifted his wings and flew away.

ᚦᛖ ᚱᛚᛏᛗᚨᚲᛗᚱ

11
The cauldron

'Why aren't we going faster?' said Dúngal. 'Isn't your friend supposed to control the wind?'

'He can't when he's in a shape-change,' said Thora.

'Then I wish he'd hurry.'

Thora glanced hopefully at Oddo, but his boy shape still gazed unseeing ahead of him.

Dúngal yawned loudly. Twilight was closing around them.

'One of us'll have to stay awake,' warned Thora, 'and look after the fire.' Dúngal leaned back, and closed his eyes. 'I guess it'll be me,' said Thora.

As the world beyond the boat disappeared into darkness, the little fire seemed to glow brighter. The boat bobbed and dipped, the dancing flames picking out a flutter of sail, a glimpse of Dúngal's cheek resting on his hand, and the glitter of water on Hairydog's fur.

Thora caught a glimpse of a sleeping gannet resting on the waves, then it was swallowed up in the night as they sailed past.

Gradually the sky lightened, and Dúngal opened his eyes.

'Oddo back yet?'

Thora shook her head.

'I'm hungry.' He scrambled to his feet, rocking the boat as he tugged at a dried fish dangling from the stay. 'Catch!' he shouted.

Thora tried, but she was numb and stiff. The fish slipped through her fingers and Hairydog snapped it up.

'Too slow.'

The hours dragged, and Dúngal fiddled impatiently, adjusting the sail, tightening knots, and checking the horizon every five minutes for a sign of land.

The wind swelled and it began to rain. Thora leaned protectively over the cauldron.

'Hurry up, Oddo,' she called. But there was no sign from the still figure at the foot of the mast.

'How fast can a bird fly?' asked Dúngal.

Thora shrugged. 'It could take ages.'

The second night, neither of them slept. Thora knew that Dúngal too was peering into the gloom, vainly trying to see what lay ahead. His ears, like hers, would be straining to hear any sound that might warn them they were nearing a shore.

There was the distant shriek of a seabird. For one hopeful moment Thora thought it might be Oddo, then she remembered that she wouldn't hear him.

Dawn was breaking. Thora glanced at Dúngal. His hair and the fur blanket around his shoulders were sparkling with tiny beads of moisture. She looked over the side of the boat. A mist clung around them, but it was slowly lifting. She saw seaweed swirling in the water beside them, the dark shapes of rocks, and then . . .

'Land!'

As they drew closer, the blurry outline took on the shape of scattered islands. They could see a jagged coastline and the white crests of surf pounding against the cliffs.

'Uch, look at those waves,' said Dúngal nervously. His voice was almost drowned by the buffeting wind and the cries of seabirds.

Thora hugged Hairydog tight, and eyed the cliffs. 'Where can we make a landing?'

Dúngal pointed to a channel running between two islands. 'We'll head over there,' he yelled.

As he steered towards the gap, the little curach was snatched up by the tidal stream and hurled between the islands. The wind, funnelled through the cliffs, rose to a screech. The water bubbled and heaved as if it was boiling in a cauldron.

Clinging to the pitching boat, Thora searched for somewhere to land.

'There!' She pointed eagerly at a pebbled beach.

Dúngal leaned on the steering oar. Nothing happened.

'It won't steer!' he shouted. He pulled at the leather bindings, and they came away, broken and useless in his hand. 'Get the sail down!'

They tore at the lines, while spray lashed their faces and the wind howled and tugged. But even without the pull of the sail, the current spun them helpless past the little bays and tiny sheltered beaches. Jagged rocks reared out of the water, and Thora felt the little boat thump and grind against them.

'We've got to stop,' she wailed.

She could see sheep grazing in meadows, houses with smoke drifting upwards, and people shouting and waving. And then they reached the last beach, the last few rocks, the last glimpse of land, and they were out of the channel and back in the open sea.

'I don't believe it!' Thora gazed back at the Isles of Faer dropping behind them. 'We went right past!'

Dúngal snatched up the oars. 'I'll row us back!'

'Wait, I'll help. Don't try . . .'

Before she could reach him, a wave tore the oars from his hands. Thora thumped the side of the boat, tears of anger and frustration burning her eyes.

'I said to *wait*.'

'Don't worry. I'll get them back. I can swim.'

Dúngal hurled himself into the sea, and immediately vanished below a wave. By the time he rose again, coughing and spluttering, the oars were tiny sticks in the distance. Thora flung a rope towards him.

'Dúngal, they're too far! You can't reach them.'

For an agonising moment, Dúngal hung on the end of the rope, gazing after the bobbing oars, then he turned and hauled himself aboard. The curach tilted alarmingly and the sea poured in. Thora just had time to catch Hairydog by the tail before the dog was swept over the side.

'You *idiot*.' Thora glared balefully at Dúngal sitting there with water streaming off his hair and clothes. 'You could have drowned. And you nearly tipped over the boat!'

At that moment, Hairydog raised her head to the sky, the ruff at her neck lifting in the wind, and gave an urgent howl.

Oddo scanned the sea, eager for a sign of the curach. He'd been flying two days and nights without rest, but he'd found Ireland, and now he could stop being a bird. The muscles in his wings were aching. And he was hungry, too. Those bullying skuas never let him eat anything. Every time he caught a fish, they snatched it away.

He looked enviously at a flock of gannets diving for their food.

'I wish I'd chosen a big bird like that for my shape-change.'

The thought had barely crossed his mind when a fountain of energy surged through him. He rolled his eyes and saw he now had long snowy wings tipped with black.

'I've turned into a gannet!' He steered towards a skua and felt a thrill of triumph as it darted out of his way. '*Now* I'll be able to eat.'

He glanced at the horizon, and saw a cluster of knobbly shapes against the smooth line of the sea. The Isles of Faer! Oddo sped towards them, dancing on the updrafts from the billowing waves. In a moment, he was circling, straining for the sound of Hairydog's bark or the ring of Thora's laughter. He spotted the little curach, bobbing on the waves beyond the islands. Shrieking with relief, he dived towards it.

There was Thora, and the cauldron . . . In a moment he would see the flames. Now he could change back to a boy! In a flurry of feathers, he dropped onto the masthead and peered excitedly downwards. He stared, and blinked, unable to believe his eyes.

He was vaguely aware of Hairydog scrambling to her feet, whining up at him, the ruff at her neck lifted by the wind. He saw Thora tilt her head, following the dog's gaze. Her hair too was blowing wildly, and she reached up her hands to clutch at the strands streaming across her eyes.

'Oddo, are you up there?' she called. Her voice sounded hoarse. 'Please, speak to me.'

Oddo stared at the tears running down her cheeks. He opened his beak. A feeble squawk trickled out, but of course, Thora couldn't hear.

She would never be able to hear him again.

The cauldron was toppled on its side, seawater sloshing in and out with every roll of the boat.

The fire was gone.

⟨ᚨᚾ ᛗᚨᚠ⟨

12
Storm

'Can't you light a new fire?' Dúngal propped up the cauldron and looked at it hopefully.

Thora stared at him, then threw herself at the sodden mess in the pit of the boat.

'Help me find the fire-lighting tools.' But there was no sign of them. She sank back, sagging in despair.

'Uch, they must have gone overboard,' said Dúngal in a small voice.

'In this tarn of a boat, there's nothing to use for tinder anyway.' Thora slapped a dripping fur blanket, then spluttered in disgust as water sprayed in her face. 'Everything's drenched.'

'I think the dippers have gone too,' said Dúngal

glumly. 'But don't worry. I can bail with my hands. I have big hands.'

He began to scoop, but most of the water trickled from his fingers before he could pour it over the side of the boat. Resignedly, Thora began to help. By the end of the day, both of them had strips of skin peeling off white, swollen palms, but the motion of the boat was a bit less sluggish.

'See?' said Dúngal. 'We'll be fine. Don't worry. I'll look after you. You want . . . uisce? Water?'

He picked up the goatskin bag and held it out. Thora took a sip.

'Yuck! Seawater's got in here too.' Suddenly, her tongue felt as dry as a salt herring. 'How are we going to manage without water? It might be days before we land anywhere and get more.'

She looked at Dúngal. He was hunched and crest-fallen.

'It's my fault, isn't it?' he said.

Thora let out a sigh and rested her head against his shoulder. They were both silent, staring at the endless waves. Thora longed for nightfall. Longed for the excuse to lie down, close her eyes and forget. But in this strange, lost world the sun sank so slowly in the sky, it seemed that night would never come.

When Thora woke, Dúngal was poking at the mess in the bottom of the boat.

'Uch, there's nothing to eat,' he muttered.

'Don't be silly, there must be!'

But Dúngal was right. The dried meat, carrots and cheese had been washed overboard, and all that was left of the bread was a few soggy crumbs tangled in the fur of the blankets.

'I'm starving!' moaned Thora.

At that moment, there was a whistling, flapping noise over her head. She looked up, startled, and just had time to duck out of the way before a fish hurtled out of the sky and landed *splat* in the curach.

'Oddo!' whispered Thora.

Dúngal looked at the fat mackerel, its blue-green scales glistening in the sunlight as it flopped around the boat.

'I thought you said he changed into a bird.'

'No, *no*! I mean Oddo caught that fish for us. Oddo's a bird. And he's brought us some food. He must be flying near us, listening and watching. And . . .' She gulped, and gazed upwards. 'He's . . . looking after us. Oh Oddo, I'm sorry about your fire.'

'Hey, thank you for the fish,' called Dúngal. 'I'll cut it up, so we can eat it.'

He reached towards Oddo's limp body, still sitting by the mast, and eased the dagger from his belt. Thora laid a portion of fish on the palm of her hand, held it in the air, and concentrated fiercely. 'Oddo, you share it with us!'

A shiver of wind brushed her cheek, and the fish was gone. Thora looked at her empty palm. 'Oh Oddo, I wish I could see you!'

She turned round and stared miserably at the empty shell of a boy who used to be Oddo. 'I'm sorry,' she whispered again.

He didn't move or blink.

A gust of wind whipped up the waves and the boat lurched uncomfortably. Thora ducked as a spray of salty water blew in her face.

'Get the sail up!' cried Dúngal, leaping to his feet. 'We're going to find land.'

'But . . . where?' yelled Thora, tugging at the tangle of lines and cloth. 'We don't know which way to go.'

'It doesn't matter. Anywhere! Where the wind takes us! I'm going to find water. And food.'

The sodden, heavy sail flapped in their faces, and the ropes bit into their hands. But at last the sail rose and the little boat took off across the water.

'Bet I'm the first to spot land,' shouted Dúngal.

Thora tucked her painful, frozen fingers under her armpits and turned her gaze towards the sea. On and on they sailed, both of them scouring the grey ripples for any sign of land.

'Ced sin?' yelled Dúngal. 'What is that?' But it was only the hump of a whale.

Thora slumped back, and closed her eyes. All she could think about was her parched throat. Her lips were swollen and cracked. When she tried to lick them, there was no moisture on her tongue.

She lost track of time. Sometimes when she opened her eyes the world was dark, and sometimes it was bright with sunshine. Dúngal had stopped chattering and fidgeting, and the only sounds were the creaking of the boat, the thump of waves, and the moaning of the wind.

'Thora, look!'

Thora's eyes sprang open. The sky was the livid purple of a bruise. Clouds thick and grey as dirty fleece were streaming across it. And stacked along the rim of the sea were misty shapes that looked like mountains.

'Is that land?'

Thora staggered to her feet, grasping the mast to steady herself. As she strained her eyes to see, the wind broke into a strange, high-pitched whine. The waves began to rush helter-skelter, piling on top of each other. The whine changed to a howling gale, and the waves reared higher and higher. Thora caught a glimpse of water rippling like an avalanche towards them. She felt the mast bending and straining, dragged by the force of a heavy, wet sail.

'Dúngal! Help me get the sail down. The mast's going to break!'

One of the ropes snapped and Thora gave a cry as it whipped across her face. Nursing her cheek, eyes smarting with tears, she watched Dúngal hack at the other lines holding the sail.

The purple cloak of the sky was ripped by a flash of lightning. A second later, thunder crashed around them. Thora could hardly think, hardly breathe. The wind battered against her, burning her face with cold. Crawling and sobbing, she gathered ropes in her hands.

'Tie . . . to the mast,' she gasped.

She began to wind a rope round Oddo's limp body, and the shivering bundle that was Hairydog. Icy water poured over her head, and she felt Dúngal grab the other rope, drag her close, and bind them both to the mast.

The boat hurtled on. Through raw, throbbing eyes Thora saw a cliff loom in front of them. The next instant they were sucked into a turmoil of thundering surf, and the curach crashed and juddered against the black, gleaming rocks. The mast tore from its footing. The bindings ripped, and Thora, clutching Oddo, was flung into the air.

She had a glimpse of purple sky, of leaping green surf, then she was plunged into icy, churning water. She flailed her legs, trying to push upwards, but Oddo's helpless body was dragging her down. The sea poured into her nose and throat, choking her, drowning her. Then, for an instant, her load seemed to lighten. She felt herself rising. There was a moment of relief, one gulp of air, and then a breaker, surging up, hurled her towards the black, jagged cliffs.

ᚱᛟᛏᛋ ᛟᚠ

13
Shipwreck

Dúngal opened his eyes. He was lying face down on a beach. A wave poured over his head, then melted away, and the white bubbles of spume sank into the wet black sand around him.

His belly gave a heave and seawater poured out of his throat.

Another breaker rolled towards him. Retching and gulping, he struggled to his hands and knees and began to crawl up the beach. The broken end of the rope around his waist trailed behind. To his right reared the huge shadow of a cliff.

'Thora?' he called.

His cry was blown away by the wind and rain. He turned to look for the curach, but all he could see was empty sand. He stumbled to his feet and began to run, tripping and scrambling, across the beach. He reached the cliffs and searched frantically among the shadowy hollows and the stony shards. But there was no movement; no answer to his cries. Only the eerie scream of gulls.

Wrapping his arms around his wet, shivering body, he huddled against the rocks, feeling as lonely and helpless as a hatchling fallen from its nest. Rain pelted his face. He tilted back his head and opened his mouth, but only a few tantalising drops landed on his parched tongue. In desperation, he turned and licked the wet, glistening surface of the cliff.

It tasted of salt.

He slumped back and gazed across the cove.

'I'm the only one left,' he thought.

There was no sign of any people. No boats, no fishing nets. Nothing. Only a black void of sand and pebbles, and then more jagged rocks, more cliffs. In front of him, the pounding waves rolled empty and relentless towards the shore. He picked up a fistful of shiny pebbles, and hurled them across the beach.

There was a beating of wings as a cluster of kitti-wakes, paddling in the spume, rose, startled, into the air. They coasted on the wind, circling and screeching. But on the rocks below, one pale wing still lifted and dipped, lifted and dipped. Dúngal watched it, puzzled. Then suddenly hope spurted through him. Maybe it wasn't a bird. Maybe . . .

He leapt to his feet and began to run. And now he could see, draped across the rocks, a grimy, tattered cloth. His sail! Once again, a corner lifted in the wind, and beneath it he caught a glimpse of small, white toes.

'*Thora!*'

He lurched forward, grabbed the edge of the sail, and yanked. Oddo was sprawled there, and beyond him, her fingers still twined around his belt, was Thora. She was lying against the boulders, her wet hair trailing like seaweed, her eyes closed.

'Uch, Thora!' Dúngal gripped her shoulder and shook. Thora's head rolled and she let out a groan. Then her eyes flickered open. She stared at him.

'Where's Oddo?' she whispered.

Dúngal pointed beside her. 'There. You're holding onto him!'

She turned to look, then let go of the belt, and rubbed her fingers. Shakily, she sat up.

At that moment, a wave slid up the beach. It curled around their legs and washed over Oddo's face. 'Help!' Thora lifted Oddo's head. 'We've got to move him.'

Oddo's limp body felt as heavy as a whale's. Slowly, painfully, they eased him a short way up the beach, and paused, panting for breath. 'All right, one more heave.'

Dúngal gritted his teeth, dug in his fingers and yanked. Oddo slid across the stones and ground to a halt. Dúngal and Thora collapsed beside him.

'I'll never move again,' groaned Dúngal.

From the corner of his eye, he saw Thora struggle to sit up. He saw her stretch an arm to something green on the cliff above her head.

'Dúngal?' she croaked. 'Can you reach? It's sea fennel. Good to eat.'

He looked. He imagined the sweet juice running down his throat. Somehow he rose to his knees, and a moment later the two of them were greedily sucking the liquid from the long, fleshy leaves.

'Better,' said Thora. 'Only . . .' She frowned round, and then began to crawl across the sand. Dúngal gazed after her, but he had about as much energy as a strand of seaweed. He sank down and closed his eyes.

He was woken by the sound of crunching. A strong, sweet perfume drowned out the smells of sea and salt. Dúngal eased one eye open.

'Want some?' Thora was chewing on a thick, purple stem, while yellow juice dripped down her chin. 'Angelica. It will make you feel better.'

Dúngal struggled to sit up and held out his hand. Thora was right. As he chewed, his body tingled back to life. In a few minutes he even felt strong enough to stand. He took a few tentative steps and grinned in delight. His legs felt almost normal. He glanced out to sea. A little head with perky black ears was bobbing on the surf.

'Hey, look!'

The wave swept up the beach, and a wet, spiky bundle dropped onto the sand. It staggered to its feet, gave a feeble shake and tottered towards them.

'Hairydog!' Thora threw her arms around the shivering creature and offered her some leaves. 'We're all together again!' she hooted. 'And we're all safe.'

'But . . . We're stuck here,' stammered Dúngal, 'with no boat. And Oddo . . . He's still . . .' He looked at the blank, staring face.

'Then we'll *get* a boat. And a fire.'

'How?' Dúngal looked around the empty cove. '*Where?*'

'There must be some people in this place,' said Thora. She pointed across the sand, and for the first time Dúngal noticed a patch of grass beyond the cove. 'I reckon that's a farm.' She scrambled to her feet. 'Let's go and look. Hairydog, you stay with Oddo.'

'Wait!' Dúngal snatched up a length of driftwood and hefted it in his hand. 'You take one too.'

'What for?'

'How do we know the people will be friendly?'

'But . . . Oh, all right.'

They hurried past the walls of the cliffs, their feet scrunching on the sand and pebbles. Then they stepped out onto springy grass.

ᛉᛋᚠᛗᚱᛗᛁᛏ ᚱᛁᛏᛋ.

14
Ice and fire

'Look at this perfect farmland,' breathed Thora.

Stretching in all directions were lush, rolling meadows, flowers and trees. And dozens of little streams glinting in the sun.

'Water!'

As they ran, laughing, across the grass, the cries of songbirds seemed to echo their excitement. Thrushes and redwings flitted between the trees. The rain stopped, and the sun shimmered in a golden, hazy sky.

They threw themselves at the nearest brook and scooped up the water, handful after handful, and poured it into their mouths.

'Stop! What was that?'

Thora hesitated, water trickling between her fingers. 'What?'

'The stream. It . . . sort of . . . spurted up.'

Thora frowned. 'I can't see anything.'

They waited. She shrugged. 'Must have been a fish or something. Anyway,' she shook the water from her hands, 'we've had enough. Let's find that fire.'

She stood up and looked around for a tell-tale wisp of chimney smoke, but all she could see was grass and trees.

'Where are all the people?' Dúngal demanded. 'And the houses? And the animals?'

'They must be further away,' said Thora. 'Come on.'

Following the river, they began to march forward. A low, snow-covered mountain hove into sight. It looked like a beast with outstretched paws, crouching behind the grassy hillocks. 'We should climb up there. If we're higher, we'll be able to see more.'

The river led them towards the mountain. As they drew close, the grey rock face took on a greenish tinge and seemed to glow strangely where it caught the light.

Dúngal turned to Thora and held out his stick.

'Hold this while I climb,' he said.

He thrust his toe in a crevice and launched himself upwards. But as his fingers touched the surface, he gave a cry and slithered to the ground.

'What's the matter?' Thora stretched out her hand to the lumpy cliff face, then drew it back in shock. 'It's not rock. It's ice!'

Their eyes followed the line of grey right up to the snow on its peak.

'What is it?' whispered Dúngal.

'It's a glacier,' said Thora. 'And that,' she pointed to the river at their feet, 'is the ice melting.'

Dúngal flung out his arms. 'Is this whole land made of ice?'

'Don't be silly.' Thora prodded the riverbank with her stick. 'Look, there's soil here.'

There was a low rumble deep under the ground. Thora dropped her stick and stumbled backwards. The river gave a leap, and a stream of water shot into the air.

'What is it? What's happening?'

The water heaved again, gave a loud hiss and erupted into foul-smelling bubbles. Then the whole river swirled downwards in a whirlpool, and disappeared. A huge black hump bubbled out of the hole, and gushed up in a jet of mud.

The ground rumbled again, and Thora could feel it trembling under her feet. The mountain of ice began to quiver. Steam snaked out of crevices and swirled around them. With a thunderous *cra-a-ack*, the peak of the glacier split open, and red and yellow flames, high as the sky, spurted upwards.

Thora couldn't move. She could hear Dúngal yelling, but the heat and noise wound around her. Her eyes were glued to the roaring, exploding fire.

Fire!

84

If any fire had the power to free Oddo from a spell, it was this one.

Dúngal was still holding his driftwood. Thora snatched it from his hand, and looked up desperately at the high, leaping flames. She had to set the stick alight. She *had* to get closer to the fire.

Underfoot, the ground heaved and ruptured. Choking clouds of steam and ash poured outwards. Thora hurled herself at the slithery surface and tried to climb, slipping and sliding.

Dúngal grabbed her from behind, and her sleeve ripped as he pulled her back.

'Leave me alone!' she yelled. 'I have to get the fire. For Oddo!'

'No!'

She could see his lips move but she couldn't hear his voice above the roar. Red-hot rocks were shooting into the air and raining around them. Thora watched as they bounded across the blackened ground, fizzing and smoking, and then the distant grass erupted into flame. With a cry, she let go of the ice and raced towards the blazing grass. She thrust in her branch, and with a jubilant whoop, waved it in the air.

'I've got the fire!'

But as she spun round in triumph, she saw the mass of ice tremble and crack. Huge chunks began to break away, and then a roiling torrent of water burst out of the glacier. Dúngal seized her hand and they fled across a ground that shook and rumbled. All they could hear was the thunder of water and the roar of fire. Thora's breath rasped in her throat. Her eyes were blinded by smoke and ash. She tripped, and plunged full-tilt into a shallow brook, holding up one arm to save her burning branch. Dúngal flopped beside her and they crouched in the middle of the swirling water.

'I think . . . we're far enough. We're safe now,' gasped Dúngal.

Thora crawled out of the water and took a deep, shuddering breath. The air was acrid with smoke, but her clothes were dripping and cool, and the grass was soft under her knees.

She turned and stared at the scene behind them.

Fire spurted from a crack in the glacier. Above it, a dense cloud of grey belched towards the sky. And below – the very ocean itself seemed to be gushing out of the ice. Whole trees, waving desperate branches, were ripped out by their roots and swept up in the torrent. Rocks and mud, trees and ice bobbed and spun in the violent flood that poured down the slope. Thora watched it surge forward, wiping out everything in its path. It pounded towards the coast, towards the quiet little cove of sand and pebbles, where . . .

'Oddo!' cried Thora. 'And Hairydog!'

She sprang to her feet. Oddo was lying helpless, in the path of the flood. She took one step, then stopped, gazing in despair at the endless, thundering stream of water.

'I can't do anything,' she wailed. She looked at the wood still burning in her hand and flung it to the ground. 'This fire's no use to him now! He'll be drowned!'

ᚦᛁᛋ ᛁᛋ ᚦᛖ ᚱᛚᚾᛏ

15
The cave

Dúngal picked up the torch.

'We'll be wanting this ourselves,' he said. 'To warm up.'

He led her across the grass. She was vaguely aware of him piling up sticks, lighting a fire, wrapping his wet cloak around her shoulders. But she couldn't stop shivering. He squatted on the ground by her side, took her hands, and held them towards the heat.

'Does that feel better?'

Better? She could never feel better. Oddo was drowned. Drowned.

'It's my fault, isn't it?' Dúngal said. 'My fault he's drowned. My fault he got stuck as a stupid bird. If it wasn't for me, he'd never even have done a shape-change.'

She couldn't answer. She lay down, but the uneasy rumbling of the earth pulsed against her ear, reminding her over and over of the flood pounding down the slope and sweeping up Oddo's helpless body. When she closed her eyes she could still see the endless flow of silver under the red glare of the flames.

In the morning, she was so stiff she couldn't move. Clouds of smoke still billowed from the glacier, and the draining floodwaters had left waves of thick grey mud across the ground. Glistening blocks of ice, half-submerged, poked from the mire among the twisted shapes of broken trees.

Dúngal was asleep, his head pillowed on dead leaves. He was covered from head to toe in fine grey ash and there were tear streaks running down his cheeks. He rolled towards her and his eyes opened.

'We have to . . . go and look,' she said huskily.

He nodded and held out his hand.

Silently they crossed the grass. The glacier was still smoking. As they drew closer, they found themselves treading in a thick layer of warm ash that puffed around them in grey clouds. The air filled with a stench like thousands of rotten eggs.

Dúngal held his nose, but Thora marched forward, her jaw stuck out, her eyes stinging with tears.

The cove came into sight and Dúngal's grip tightened on her hand.

Thora stared at the desolation. Even the beach of sparkling black pebbles had disappeared. There was nothing now but a thick layer of dull grey sludge. There was no sign that Oddo or Hairydog had ever been there. She stepped forward, the mud sucking at her feet.

A frenzy of ecstatic yipping broke out overhead. Thora threw back her head and saw, poking from the cliff, a familiar muzzle.

'*Hairydog!*' Tears blurred her eyes and laughter bubbled in her chest. Next moment, she was running and stumbling through the ooze. 'Hairydog, Hairydog!'

She reached the cliff and stretched up on her toes, but she could not touch the ledge where the dog was standing.

'Come on, girl, jump!'

Hairydog turned and vanished into a cave behind her, whining and barking.

'Come on, it's not far.'

Dúngal joined her.

'The silly dog won't jump. She must have scrambled into that cave when she saw the flood, and now she won't come down again!'

'Maybe she's still frightened.'

Thora glowered at the crumbling rock face.

'Well, I can't climb up to *her*,' she said, exasperated. The foot of the cliff had been carved away by the force of the flood.

'Try this, then.' Dúngal began to build a heap of stones and mud. 'Stand on that and see if you can reach her.'

Thora placed a foot on top of the pile, grasped a jutting rock and pushed upwards. Her eyes came level with the ledge. She could see Hairydog, and behind her, in the darkness, something lying on the floor of the cave. She strained forward, trying to see what it was. Hairydog gave it a nudge and it rolled over. An arm flopped into sight.

Thora felt her strength drain away. She stumbled off the rocks to the ground.

'Dúngal,' she gasped. 'Dúngal, there's . . . there's someone . . . inside!'

Thora was shaking so much she could hardly stand. She wrapped her arms around herself as Dúngal leapt onto the pile of stones and hoisted himself up to the ledge. She heard him scramble forward. There was a hollow yell from inside the cave, then his face popped out again, pink and excited.

'It's Oddo,' he yelled, 'and I think he's alive!'

Thora sat down with a *plop* in the mud. Oddo wasn't drowned! Hairydog must have dragged him into the cave. He was here. He was safe. And now—

'The fire!' she gasped. 'I'll fetch the fire.'

Gathering her muddy skirts in her hand, she flew back to the meadow. A few wispy flames still danced among the blackened sticks. Thora puffed frantically till

91

they flared up, seized a burning willow branch and carried it to the beach.

Dúngal was waiting in front of the cave. Eagerly, Thora held up the torch. He took it, then hesitated.

'What'll I do with it?'

Thora stared. She had no idea. She looked around wildly, as if the cauldron might suddenly appear again.

'Maybe . . . just hold it near him,' she said at last.

Dúngal crawled back into the cave, and Thora climbed onto the heap of stones and peered over the ledge.

The interior of the cave was a confusion of leaping shadows and glowing orange light. Behind the black shape of Dúngal's crouching figure, she could see the top of Oddo's head and his sprawling legs.

He wasn't moving.

Thora clenched the edge of the rock and held her breath.

ᚼᛁ ᚲᚨᚼ ᚲᚨᚱᛒ

16
The light in the rock

Oddo the gannet hovered over the ghastly mess of broken trees and grey mud covering the beach. A girl was stumbling across the soggy ground with a dog leaping and barking beside her. Oddo wanted to flee, high up in the air like the other birds, but in the girl's hand was something that glowed and shimmered like a piece of sun torn from the sky; and it was drawing him down . . . down . . .

For an instant, it lit up an archway of rock, then disappeared into the cliff. With every nerve tense, Oddo plunged after it. He felt jagged edges tear at his wings; he saw a bright glow fill the air around him. Then his body lost all weight, all feeling.

Oddo opened his eyes. A boy was crouched over him,

with a burning stick in his hand. Oddo stared at the dark eyes, the bare face, the crest of red-brown feathers on top of the head. No – not feathers, hair! It was . . .

Oddo jerked upright, banging his head against the overhanging stone, just as Dúngal blurted a warning.

Rubbing his head, Oddo rolled over, and saw Thora's eyes staring at him over the edge of the rock.

Oddo grinned. That felt strange. He wasn't used to having a mouth instead of a beak.

He stopped rubbing his head and inspected his hands. A pebble rattled. Oddo looked at it, then picked it up – delicately, between two fingers. He heaved a satisfied sigh, then prodded Dúngal on the knee.

'Aren't you going to let me out of here?' he asked. As Dúngal scrambled backwards, Oddo wriggled across the rock and slid off the edge. Instinctively, he raised his arms, then let out an exclamation of surprise as he dropped like a stone. Shocked, he squatted where he landed, his feet sunk in the mud. He felt massive and heavy and awkward.

A blur hurtled towards him and knocked him onto his back. He squirmed as Hairydog slathered his face with wet doggy kisses. A moment later, he felt Thora's arms twine around and hold him tight. He hugged her back, then sat up. She gazed at him, snivelling and beaming at the same time.

Then he looked at Dúngal.

'Oddo, I'm sorry,' said the Irish boy. 'I—'

'Oh Oddo-o-o,' Thora butted in, 'when that fire in the cauldron went out, I thought I'd never, ever speak to you again!' And then she glowered. 'I *knew* it wasn't safe to do a shape-change without a wand! Especially after you chopped that tree without asking permission.'

'Well, I got back in the end!' said Oddo. The mud made a loud sucking gurgle as he wrenched himself free and stood up. 'Do you know where we are?'

Thora shook her head.

'We haven't seen any people yet,' she said. 'We've only found that . . . that fire in the ice!'

Oddo grinned. 'Lucky you did,' he said. 'Or I'd still be stuck in a bird shape!'

↑᚛ ᛗᛁᚱᚲ ᛊᚠ

17
Search

Oddo blew on the charred snakeweed root, then with slow relish sank in his teeth. The spicy flavour filled his mouth.

'A nice change from raw fish!' he said.

He licked his fingers, then leaned against the trunk of the willow tree and stared at the others.

'Now what?' he asked. 'We've got no boat, and no idea where we are. What's your plan?'

Dúngal bent forward. 'Did you find out where Ériu is?' he demanded.

Oddo nodded and gestured to the coast.

'South,' he said.

'I *told* you that.'

Oddo opened his mouth to retort, then stopped as Dúngal blushed sheepishly.

'Sorry,' muttered Dúngal. 'You're right. I wasn't really sure. And . . . thank you . . . for looking.'

'Well, anyway,' said Thora, 'now we know for sure. So all we need is a new boat.' She stood up, her old determined self again. 'We'll go find the people who live here. They'll have boats.'

Dúngal snatched a burning stick from the campfire. 'I'll bring the fire!'

They stepped out, following the range of mountains to their right. They crossed stepping stones reflected in clear streams, and saw peaks of glaciers glinting in the sun. They passed through meadows where snipe and golden plovers scratched among the pink and purple flowers. They found a waterfall so high it seemed to pour from the clouds, and a forest where meadow pipits and redwings clamoured in the trees.

'This place is rather nice,' mused Thora, 'when it's not bursting into flames or flood.'

'But . . . where are the people?' Oddo demanded. In their hours of walking, they'd seen no sign of any farm, or animal, or person.

All through the afternoon and the long, twilit evening they kept on moving.

'Lucky the days are so long here,' said Thora.

Oddo sighed. He was beginning to fear they would never find what they were looking for. Maybe there *weren't* any people living here. And he was tired and hungry. He kept stealing glances at Dúngal, but the Irish boy was marching stolidly forward, his face lit by the torch in his hand, while the world around them dissolved into a grey blur.

Oddo gritted his teeth. 'I'm not giving up before he does.'

At last he saw Dúngal hesitate and yawn. Oddo didn't need another cue.

'It's no use walking in the dark,' he called.

He flopped where he stood, on the soft grass of a meadow, and sank immediately into a deep sleep.

It seemed only a minute later when someone shook his shoulder.

'What is it?' he groaned, and opened an eye.

Thora was leaning over him.

'It's pouring!' she complained. 'And the fire's gone out.'

Oddo mumbled at the rain to go away, then tried to roll over. But Thora didn't let go.

'Get up,' she insisted. 'It's light enough to see again!' While Oddo staggered to his feet, Thora headed off across the meadow. 'Come on, you lazy limpets!' she called back over her shoulder.

Oddo turned to see Dúngal struggling blearily to his knees. The two of them looked at each other, and at the same instant rolled their eyes. For the first time, Oddo felt a spark of kinship with this strange boy.

As they stumbled side by side through the dewy grass, an eider duck, quacking crossly, flew up almost from beneath their feet. On the ground behind her, in a nest of soft grey down, lay three yellow eggs.

'Breakfast!' they shouted together. 'Hey, Thora!'

They paused just long enough to let the raw yolk slither down their throats, and, as they hurried on, Oddo thought longingly of hot porridge and fresh-made bread dripping with butter.

Racing ahead, Thora leapt onto a rock and came to a halt.

'Hey!' she called. 'There's a river here.'

Hairydog, yapping with excitement, bounded up beside her, then disappeared. When Oddo and Dúngal reached the bank, the dog was already halfway across. She scrambled out the other side, shook the water from her fur, and grinned in triumph.

'Our turn,' said Thora. Grabbing rocks and over-hanging branches, she slithered, fully clothed, down the bank. 'Come on, you chicken-legs!' She turned and splashed the others with the icy water.

Oddo glanced at Dúngal.

'Right.'

Together they leapt off the rock, and jumped in with a big splash, right next to Thora.

Oddo gasped as the freezing water poured over him. The current almost shoved him off his feet. Dúngal yelled, and Oddo just managed to snatch hold of his tunic before he disappeared under the foam. Thora gripped his sleeve, and the three of them, clinging together, inched across the river and clambered up the bank.

Dúngal gave a squeak and began to dance around. There was something flapping inside his tunic.

'Undo your belt!' cried Thora.

They all watched in astonishment as a trout wiggled out and plopped to the ground.

Thora dived on it. 'We'll eat this later.'

'Raw,' sighed Oddo.

They set off again, but there was no happy chatter now, just the *slosh slosh* of dripping clothes. Soon Oddo's legs were chafed and sore from the wet breeches. He drooped his head, not bothering to look where he was going. They weren't going to find any people or boats. There was no one living here.

Thora's voice broke the silence. 'What's that?' She sounded anxious.

Oddo glanced up. There were wisps of smoke or steam weaving through the trees ahead of them.

'It's not one of those glaciers erupting again, is it?'

The three of them hesitated, then edged cautiously forward, expecting every minute to feel the earth explode under their feet. The haze wrapped around them, dense and moist, filling their nostrils with the stink of rotten eggs. All they could hear was the swish of their own feet through soft, dead leaves. All they could see were the ghostly shapes of trees looming abruptly in front of their faces.

Suddenly Thora gave a cry and stepped back. Ahead of them, the ground dropped away. At their feet, half hidden by the cover of white, swirling mist, lay a lake of deep turquoise blue.

'That's not a glacier,' whispered Oddo.

Dúngal dropped onto the bank and slid his toes into the water. He let out a yelp and jerked his legs upwards.

'It's hot!' he cried.

'What do you mean?'

Thora and Oddo knelt down and cautiously dipped in their fingers. They stared at each other in astonishment.

'It *is* hot,' spluttered Thora.

'Let's get in!' said Dúngal.

A moment later, with squeaks and gasps, all three of them eased themselves into the steaming bath.

'It's . . . certainly . . . hot,' panted Oddo.

He bounced up and down, his feet digging into the gravelly bottom, so that tongues of heat gushed out of the ground. Hairydog, half hidden by wisps of steam, yapped anxiously from the shore.

A few minutes were enough for Oddo. He scrambled out, with Thora close on his heels, but Dúngal was determined to stay in longer. When he crawled out at last, his face was dripping with sweat and his skin was red and shiny.

'You're practically boiled,' said Oddo. 'I reckon that water's hot enough for cooking.'

'Let's try!' Thora exclaimed. 'Here's the fish!'

A short time later, they were sitting on the bank, watching the fat trout simmer in the steaming lake.

Thora shook her head in disbelief. 'I don't believe this place!' she said. 'Hot water that comes out of the ground. Fish that want to be caught. It's the best land in the world!'

'Not as good as Ériu,' growled Dúngal. 'In Ériu we don't have mountains made of ice that spit fire and rocks. We—'

'But Ériu's already full of people!' said Oddo. 'Look at this place. All this empty land! You could build a house anywhere you wanted.'

'And you'd never have to worry about Grimmr the Greedy stealing your land.'

'You wouldn't have to worry about the stupid King and his taxes, either.'

'You could bring the cows and sheep here in Farmer Ulf's longship.'

Oddo stared at Thora.

'You're serious, aren't you?' he said. 'You think we really could live here.'

Before Thora could answer, Dúngal interrupted.

'Hey,' he said, 'that trout must be cooked by now.'

Oddo hardly noticed what he was eating. He was picturing the house his father could build on the hill near the lake. He dug his finger into the ground and crumbled the soft, rich soil. He imagined a field of barley, a cowshed, a haystack . . .

'First, we have to get back to Norway and fetch our families,' said Thora.

Oddo blinked, and the vision vanished.

'How?'

'There must be someone living here – somewhere. And they've got to have a boat. Come on.'

As they set off again, the wall of mountains seemed to curve across their path. Drawing close, they saw that one mountain reared up alone from the surrounding meadows. The sun was beginning to set, but in the twilight Oddo could make out dark hollows in the rocky slopes.

'Hey, look at the caves. Let's sleep in—' His voice caught in his throat. There was something moving at the foot of the mountain. Something big. An animal . . . or a person.

They had all seen it now and they stood, frozen, as the figure detached itself from the shadow of the mountain.

ᛒᚱᚨᛒ

18
Father Connlae

'It's a woman,' breathed Oddo.

Dúngal, too, saw the long robe flowing to the ground. It was the colour of the rocks, and girded at the waist with a cord. But then he noticed the hair – long on the neck, but shaven from ear to ear.

'That's no woman!' he cried, his voice ringing in excitement. 'That's a priest!' He ran forward, shouting in his own tongue. 'A Athir! A Athir!'

The priest turned in astonishment and put out his hands to catch Dúngal as he hurtled forward.

'Fáilte!' he cried, and at the sound of the Irish greeting, Dúngal thought he would burst. 'Uch, boy, what are you doing so far from home? How came you *here*?'

Dúngal stared with delight at the shaven chin, so

different from the Vikings' long, rough beards. He looked into eyes that were the pale, transparent blue of the sky.

'I was captured by Viking raiders. I built a curach and tried to get home, but . . .' Dúngal's chin quivered and he felt tears welling up. He gulped. 'But I ended up here!'

'And who are you, child? What is your name?'

'I'm Dúngal macc Flainn of Laigin.'

'And I hail from the monastery of Cill Dara. My name is Connlae.'

Father Connlae's voice was soft and rustling, like the wind through leaves. He was a small man, elderly and shaky. His hand trembled as it rested on Dúngal's sleeve. But his face was curiously unlined, just like the abbot's at the monastery where Dúngal had learnt his letters.

Dúngal heard Thora and Oddo coming up behind him, and Hairydog's panting breath. The dog's muzzle butted his knee and he stroked her head. 'This is Hairydog, and these are my friends, Oddo and Thora. They're Vikings, but they helped me. And now, because of me, they're stranded too.' He looked around at the bulky shape of the mountain and the shadowy trees. 'What is this strange land, anyway?' he asked. 'Are there other people here from Ériu?'

Father Connlae shook his head.

'No longer. I am the only one from Ériu now. There were other Brothers with me, but they have left. For the Vikings are arriving now. Even here, in this place of peace and prayer, they find us and harass us.'

'Vikings? Where? We didn't see them!'

'No, as yet there are but few. They have settled yonder.' He lifted a trembling hand. 'In the west.'

Dúngal felt Oddo pinching his arm.

'What is it? What are you saying? What's he telling you?'

'He says there are Vikings here.'

'Here? But what *is* this place?'

Dúngal turned back to the priest and caught a puzzled expression on his face. 'You can speak to these people in their language?' he asked.

Dúngal nodded proudly. 'And they're asking you the name of this place,' he said.

'The Vikings call it Iceland.'

'*Iceland?* But what about the fire? I'd call it Fireland!'

'Yes,' said the priest. 'Buried beneath the mountains of ice, there is a heart of fire. But it is a land of bounty, too. My goats and I never want for food. The rivers teem with fish, there is endless pastureland . . . It was a haven till the dreaded Vikings came. And now, I live in fear that they will find me and make me their slave.'

'Why don't you go back to Ériu, then?'

'Uch, how I long to leave. But I have no boat. I chose to remain when the other Brothers left, and now . . .' Sadly he shook his head. 'But enough about me, you are weary and hungry. Come, bring your friends and share my supper.'

He ushered them towards a crevice in the side of the mountain, and they squeezed through to find themselves in a cave. There was dry grass on the floor, and furniture made from branches and rough-hewn logs.

'This must be his house,' whispered Thora, her voice faltering as she eyed the laden table in the middle of the room.

'Father Connlae says have biad – food!' said Dúngal.

They all dived at the table. There was a round, flat bread made from wild grass seeds, strips of dried fish topped with a sweet relish of sea fennel, and a bowl of white, lumpy curds.

Dúngal snatched up the bread and crammed most of it into his mouth at one bite.

'Hey,' said Oddo, 'how about the rest of us?'

Dúngal felt his face burning. He pulled the loaf out of his mouth. It was damp and slightly mauled.

'Sorry. Want some?'

'Not now!'

'Please don't argue. There is plenty of food.' Father Connlae heaved open a wooden chest. He drew out handfuls of shrivelled fruit, nuts and seaweed and poured them on the table. 'Here, here.' With shaky hands he thrust them towards the children. 'Eat.' He beamed and nodded, picking up titbits and pushing them into their hands whenever they paused.

'Tell him I can't eat any more!' said Thora.

'Me neither!'

The three friends collapsed on a heap of soft heather at the side of the cave.

'What's this?' Thora picked up a book lying on the floor and lifted the cover. 'It's names, like you drew in the dirt, Dúngal. *Lots* of names!'

Dúngal took the book and read a few lines.

'It's not just names. It's a story.'

'A *story*?' Thora brushed her hand over the soft, white page. 'And what's this stuff it's drawn on?'

'Skin from a . . . lóeg . . . a calf.'

Thora and Oddo looked inquisitively around the room.

'And what are those funny torches made from?' Oddo pointed at candles stuck on rocky projections around the walls.

'I . . . don't know how to say it in your tongue. It comes from the bees.'

'Is that what you have in Ireland? Why don't you just use wood, or fish oil, like we do?'

'It lasts longer, I think.'

'It smells nicer too.'

The priest was watching them talk, beaming, his head moving from side to side as each one spoke. Then the candle over Thora's head gave a sputter and began to smoke. Father Connlae rose to his feet.

'It is time to sleep.' He snuffed out the sputtering candle. 'Please, lay your heads here.' He patted the heather they were sitting on. 'And cover yourselves with these.' He handed them a bundle of goatskins, then moved around the room, snuffing the other candles.

'He says to go to sleep.' Dúngal yawned, and leaned back.

'Tomorrow,' said Thora, 'we'll find those other Vikings. And their longships!'

'No!' Dúngal shot up again. 'You can't do that! If they see me, they'll make me into a thrall again. And Father Connlae too!'

By the faint glow of a single candle, Oddo and Thora gaped at him.

'Then how are we supposed to get out of this place?'

There was no answer. The last light went out. In miserable silence, the three weary travellers lay down. They were shivering now in their cold, wet clothes. Groping in the darkness, Dúngal tugged a goatskin over himself and curled up, trying to get warm.

ᛈᛗᛁ ᛋᛚ ᚨᚱ

19
Goatskin

When Oddo opened his eyes again, he could see the dim shapes of the other sleeping figures. Daylight was trickling through the entrance, making a pale streak across the floor of the cave. Father Connlae was lying on the hard earth, his head pillowed on a rock.

'We took all his bedding!' thought Oddo guiltily. He sat up, shivering. Hastily, he pulled the goatskin around his shoulders and up over his head.

Thora stretched, yawned, and poked Dúngal.

'Where's Oddo?' she whispered.

Dúngal peered round the room.

'Maybe he went outside.'

Oddo frowned at them. 'I'm right here.'

Thora looked straight at him. 'Where?'

'Here, stupid, right next to you.'

Thora's hand wavered through the air and landed on his arm. She let out a scream.

'I can feel you, but I can't see you!' she cried. 'What have you done?'

'I haven't done anything. Look, I'm here.' Oddo stood up.

Thora blinked. 'Yes, I can see you now, but . . .' She snatched at the goatskin that was sliding off his shoulders. 'Did you just have this round your head?'

'Yes, but . . .'

Thora's eyes were very wide. 'It must have worked like Ketil's goatskin hood – you know, the one that makes him invisible.'

Oddo stared at the white, furry hide.

'Do it again!' said Dúngal.

Oddo reached out, took the skin and wrapped it around his head. From the others' expressions, he knew it had worked.

At that moment, Father Connlae grunted and sat up. Quickly, Oddo dropped the hood, feeling his cheeks flush as the priest gave him a puzzled glance. Rubbing his back, Father Connlae tottered to his feet. He caught the children watching him and smiled. His smile was reassuring, like a hand reaching out to pat their heads. Then he murmured something to Dúngal, picked up two buckets, and carried them out of the room.

'He's going to milk the . . . gaboro . . . the goats,' Dúngal explained.

'We should help,' said Oddo.

'Wait a minute.' Thora's eyes were blazing with excitement. She held the goatskin and waved it in the air. 'We've got to think of a way to use this magic,' she said.

'Well, if I'm invisible I can sneak up on people without their seeing me.'

'You could sneak up on the Vikings,' suggested Dúngal. 'Steal a longship!'

'Well, maybe not a whole big ship. But . . . a boat.'

They all looked at each other.

'Right,' said Thora, standing up. 'Dúngal, you talk to Father Connlae, find out exactly where the Vikings are. Oddo, we'll take over the milking.'

As she marched out of the room, Oddo raised his eyebrows at Dúngal. 'Yes, Captain Thora!' he whispered.

Father Connlae was crouched inside the pen with his small herd of goats. When Oddo and Thora slipped around one of the rough willow-branch hurdles, he beamed again, his warm, gentle smile, and handed them the empty bucket.

'Now, Dúngal, you ask him where we have to go!' said Thora.

'Yes, Captain,' said Dúngal.

Thora looked bewildered as Oddo and Dúngal burst into a fit of giggles.

'Well, it looks like you two are friends at last,' she said. 'What's the big joke?'

Dúngal made a face at Oddo and hurried after the priest.

'U-u-uh, just something silly,' mumbled Oddo. He wrapped his arms round one of the goats. 'You milk, while I hold her still.'

When the bucket was full, they carried it to the campfire, where the priest was dropping some brown, curly leaves into the cooking.

'Thora,' hissed Oddo, 'that stuff looks like the lichen we fed the cows – you know, that time Grimmr stole the hay.'

'So?'

Oddo bit his lip. It was all right for Thora. Even at home she ate wild food from the woods and the sea, but he was used to proper meals – oat porridge, barley bread . . . He took a bite of Father Connlae's brown leafy mush. It tasted bitter and lumpy.

He stared into the fire, remembering his last glimpse of his mother bent over the cooking pot at home. Would he ever see her again?

'Do you want more?' Thora picked up the ladle and leaned towards the cauldron.

Oddo caught his breath. For a moment, Thora looked just like his mother.

'I . . .' He couldn't answer. He just stared at her.

'Hey, you two,' interrupted Dúngal, 'Father Connlae

says the Vikings are only a few hours walk away. If we leave now, we can reach there before nightfall!'

Thora straightened and turned. Oddo blinked. With her long, silky hair and her tiny nose, how had he thought she looked like Sigrid?

'Did you ask him about the goatskin?' asked Thora.

Dúngal nodded. 'He says we can take it. I had to tell him why, though.' He eyed Oddo. 'So, he knows you're magic now.'

The priest waved to them as they set off, and called out something in a quavery, anxious voice.

'He says to make sure the Vikings don't see us,' said Dúngal.

Thora turned and waved back.

'Don't worry. We'll be careful,' she called.

Today, none of them noticed what they passed. They were all searching the distance, vying to be the first to see the Viking settlement.

In the end, it was Hairydog who found it. She reached the crest of a hill, turned back, and let out a short bark. Oddo panted up to join her, and there in the valley below he saw a long, low house roofed in turf. A man with a plaited beard was crossing the yard. He had a milking bucket in his hand, and a dog at his heels. There were cows, and sheep, and . . . It all looked so familiar, so much like home. Oddo felt warmth spreading out from his heart, reaching his throat and his eyes. Without thinking, he opened his mouth to shout a greeting.

The next thing he knew, he was flat on his back with Dúngal sitting on top of him, and Thora hanging onto Hairydog with a hand clapped around her muzzle.

'Oddo, tell her to stop barking!'

With a jolt of shock, Oddo realised he'd nearly given them all away.

'H-Hairydog,' he said. His voice came out in a croak. 'Keep quiet!'

Dúngal crawled off him, glaring ferociously, and they all crouched low, peering down the slope. There was smoke drifting from the chimney hole, and the smell of cooking wafted towards them. But all eyes were drawn to the river, where a longship, sail furled, bobbed at its mooring.

ᛁᛏ   ᛗᚨᛏᛋᛗᚱ...

20
Under the hood

'Give me the goatskin,' whispered Oddo.

Dúngal had been wearing it as a cloak, but now he handed it to Oddo.

'Good luck.'

Oddo stood up, and wrapped the goatskin carefully round his head and shoulders.

'It's working,' said Thora excitedly. 'Now make sure you keep it over your head all the time.'

When Oddo turned to go, Hairydog sprang to his side.

'No, girl, you stay here.' He watched the dog flop to the ground, and frowned anxiously. 'I think she can still see me,' he said. 'And that means the hound down there will be able to see me too!'

'So what?' said Thora. 'Just tell it to be quiet. You can talk to animals!'

Oddo tiptoed down the hill. Just near the yard, a twig snapped under his foot. The hound began to bark and the farmer peered up the hill. Oddo's hand flew to his head to check his hood was still in place. He waited, holding his breath and feeling horribly exposed, praying that Dúngal and Thora were well hidden.

'It's all very well Thora telling me to order the dog around,' he thought. 'But how can I, when the man's standing right next to it? The cloak won't make my *voice* disappear!'

He caught the dog's eye and stared at it, willing it to be quiet. The animal stopped barking, tilted its head on one side, and lay down. The farmer shrugged, and headed for the house.

Oddo crept forward again. The house was built of turf dug from the earth around it. Oddo could see the raw cuts in the ground. On the river, he could see the longship rocking gently. And tied up behind it . . . Oddo gulped. There was a small rowing boat, with oars resting ready on the benches. There was nobody in sight. Now was the perfect time to slip the moorings, and quietly row it away.

From inside the house came a clamour of Viking voices, and the tantalising odour of roasted lamb. Oddo hesitated. It was a long time since breakfast, and it would be longer yet before his feet were back in a Viking home.

'Just a quick peek,' he vowed, 'and a tiny bite. And then I'll steal the boat.'

He tiptoed along the paved path, following the farmer into a tunnel cut in the thickness of the walls. The man was just pushing his way through the skin draperies at the other end. Oddo could hear men and women laughing and talking. He took a deep breath, patted his hood again, and stepped through the door.

The scene inside was just like any farmhouse back home. Sprawled on benches around the table, a noisy crowd were eating, drinking and shouting with laughter. They were half in shadow, half lit by the lights of the flickering oil lamps. A thrall circled them, bearing a large jug, and hands rose and fell as the diners tossed back their ale and held out their horns for more. Three women bent over the firepit in the middle of the floor, faces red and perspiring as they turned a spit and heaved a heavy saucepan off the flames. Oddo's tongue watered. When one of the women started to hack slices off the haunch of meat to pile on a wooden platter, Oddo sidled closer. The instant she twisted back to the spit, his hand flashed out, snatched a piece of meat and stuffed it into his mouth.

Chewing happily, he crouched on the floor and began to listen to the rowdy conversation at the table. The hot fire made sweat trickle down the back of his neck, and he slid a finger under his hood to let in some air.

'Dyflinn's the place!' shouted a man with grey locks and a face marked by a long scar. He thumped his fist, and a bowl of whey bounced and splattered.

'That's right,' answered his neighbour. He was a pasty-faced fellow with a low, gravelly voice. 'Irish make the best thralls. I say we check out the slave market in Dyflinn.'

'What about a raid?' an eager voice piped up. 'Easy pickings anywhere in Ireland. Pick up our own thralls.'

'Hear, hear!'

Oddo sprang to his feet, quivering with rage. It was louts like these who'd kidnapped Dúngal, and dragged him to the market in chains. He glared round the table at their gloating faces.

One man glanced his way, looked puzzled, and pointed.

'Who's that boy?' he asked.

Oddo grasped his head, and to his horror felt hair instead of goatskin. The hood had fallen away and now everyone could see him.

They were silent, staring.

'I . . . I'm a Viking,' he said. 'I . . . I was on a boat and it was wrecked and . . . here I am.'

'A boat?'

'What boat?'

'Is there anyone else?'

'Where did you land?'

'What's your name?'

The questions flew at him like arrows and he stared back, feeling like a hunted animal. In his head he could still hear Dúngal's frightened cry: 'If they see me, they'll make me into a thrall again!'

'How am I going to stop them finding the others?' he thought in despair.

One of the red-faced women slapped a platter on the table and glared at the men.

'You ill-mannered boors,' she scolded. 'This poor lad must be famished and exhausted. Stop pestering him and let him sit down and eat.'

There were rumbles as the men shifted along, making a space for Oddo. He slid onto the end of a bench, head bowed, cheeks burning with embarrassment.

'There, dearie.' The woman leaned across, smelling of sweat and smoke, and handed him a wooden plate heaped with bread and meat. Oddo could feel everyone watching him. The bread filled his mouth, doughy and sticky, and he had to gulp noisily to swallow it. At last, the men turned away and began to plan their raids again.

'We should leave soon,' said one of them, 'we want to journey there and back before the summer ends.'

'And who'll stay here?' the woman demanded, as she plonked another platter on the table, straightened up, and crossed her arms. 'There's plenty to see to on the farms, and us three womenfolk can't do it all.'

There was a pause.

'Well, then, some of us will stay,' said Pasty-face.

'Hold on, not so fast!' The grey-haired man wagged his finger. 'If half the crew is stranded here, who'll man the ship?' He scowled around the table, and all the others grunted and frowned and tugged at their beards.

The grey-haired man suddenly pointed at Oddo.

'You, boy, you said you came here on a boat. Can you row? Can you sail?'

'We'll soon teach him, if he can't!'

There were hoots of laughter, and knife handles banged on the table.

Oddo stared at the leering faces, his belly churning with fear and excitement. These men were offering him passage on a boat to Ireland. Only . . . he couldn't leave Dúngal and Thora and Hairydog in this land of ice and fire. He had to find a way to take them too. He couldn't go alone!

ᚱ

21
The plan

Thora's eyes flew open. There it was again – the sound of running footsteps. She peered through the juniper branches. It was Oddo, thudding up the hill towards them. To Thora's dismay, she saw the hood had fallen from his head and was flapping behind him.

He was hurtling past, when Thora called out in a hoarse whisper, 'Oddo!' He spun round. 'Here, under the bush!'

He knelt down and peered through the juniper needles. Dúngal was awake now too, and Hairydog wriggled out to lay her head on Oddo's knee and gaze up into his face.

'Oddo, do you know your hood's fallen off?'

Oddo made a wry face. 'I know.' He glanced over

his shoulder down the hill. 'Let's get away from here, and I'll tell you what's been happening.'

When they were safe in a grove of birch trees, Oddo began to speak.

'I found out the Vikings are just about to sail. And guess where they're going!'

Thora looked at him. 'Home?'

'No-o-o.' A huge grin spread across his face. 'To Ireland!' he exploded.

'But . . . how will that help me?' said Dúngal. 'Are you thinking I can hide on the boat?'

'You won't need to,' Oddo gloated. 'They want people to join their crew. They don't have to know you're Irish. You can speak like a Viking. We'll call you . . . Dufnall.'

'What about *me*?' cried Thora. 'They won't want a girl.'

'Pretend you're a boy, then.'

Thora eyed him thoughtfully. 'My name could be Thorvald,' she said. 'And I could cut my kirtle shorter to make it into a tunic. But . . . I don't have any breeches.'

'You can have mine,' said Oddo. 'Dúngal and I will pretend we lost ours in the shipwreck.'

'What about Father Connlae?' Dúngal broke in. '*He* can't pretend to be a Viking. He doesn't know your language.'

'Father Connlae?!' Oddo squeaked. 'What *about* Father Connlae?'

'We can't leave him behind. He wants to go back to Ireland too. We have to rescue him before your horrid mates get hold of him.'

Thora could see the frustration in Oddo's face. She interrupted before he yelled at Dúngal.

'Why don't we . . .' She racked her brain desperately for an idea, and then it came. 'Why don't we pretend Father Connlae's hurt his tongue, or something, so he can't speak?'

She beamed in satisfaction.

'Don't be silly,' said Oddo.

And then Thora remembered the priest's shaven chin, and tonsured hair. Father Connlae certainly didn't look like a Viking.

'You can't lose a *beard* in a shipwreck!' said Oddo.

'He can grow a beard,' said Thora promptly. 'He just has to stop shaving.'

'He can't grow a full beard in a couple of days!'

They all stared at each other, then Thora lifted a strand of her own hair.

'We could cut this off,' she said slowly, 'and stick it on his chin.'

She looked hopefully at Oddo. He heaved a sigh and shrugged his shoulders.

'If you want, you can give it a try,' he said.

Thora bit her lip as Oddo lifted up her hair to make

the first slash. From the corner of her eye she saw the glint of the dagger, then there was a ripping sound close to her ear. She felt short ends of hair flop against her cheek, and Oddo held out a fistful of honey-coloured strands. Thora gulped.

'Next one,' said Oddo cheerily, and he grasped another clump.

A few minutes later, Thora stood up. Her neck felt cold and bare.

Dúngal pointed at the cuttings lying on the ground. 'There's Father Connlae's beard,' he chuckled.

'How are you going to stick them on his chin?' asked Oddo.

'Fish glue,' said Thora. 'I'll boil up some fishbones.'

Next morning, alone in the cave, Thora undid her bronze brooches and let her apron dress slide to the floor. She picked up the dagger and shortened the skirt of her kirtle till it hung to just above her knees. Shivering, she pulled on the breeches Oddo had given her to cover her bare legs.

'Now, a belt.' She knotted a cord around her waist. 'And . . .' She hesitated, slid the dagger into the belt and took a deep breath. 'I'm ready.' Dressed in this strange outfit, her short hair bouncing round her face, she felt like a new person – wild and daring. Heart pounding with excitement, she crossed the room, and stepped through the doorway.

'How do I look?' she called.

Nobody answered. They were busy dismantling the goat pen and shooing the animals into the woods. Thora watched Oddo running between the trees, his bare legs long and spindly like the branches of the willows.

'He's grown nearly as tall as Arni,' she realised with surprise. 'And . . . Dúngal's right, he does look like Arni!' At home, Oddo's hair was always brushed into a glossy, bronze cap, but now it was unruly and matted like her brother's.

Father Connlae toddled into view and she felt a mixture of laughter and terror bubble up inside her. She stared at the two plaits swinging from his chin and prayed the Viking raiders would believe that was a real braided beard.

ᚦᛁᛋ ᛁᛋ ᚦᛖ ᚱᚢᚾ

22
Striker

They headed down the hill towards the Viking farm. Dúngal saw the longship, sail unfurled, and the men loading her. They looked just like the raiders who'd captured him. He felt sick.

'As soon as they see my hair and my freckles, they'll know I'm Irish. They'll know I'm a thrall,' he groaned.

'Pig's piddle.' Thora took a firm grip on his sleeve. 'Farmer Ulf's got red hair, and he's a Viking. Just remember – don't say anything in Irish.'

'I'm not stupid.'

Dúngal glanced at Father Connlae. The priest's knees were white and knobbly; he had a strange woollen cowl on his shaven head, and two silly plaits dangling from his chin. But as the old man tottered down the slope, he turned to Dúngal and winked.

As they approached the house, a tall Viking appeared in the doorway. Below his shaggy grey hair, his face was puckered by a scar that ran from brow to chin.

'Ah, my new crew,' he said. 'I'm *Striker*'s captain. Snari's the name.'

Oddo drew to a halt and the others clustered behind him.

'These are my friends.' Dúngal could hear the nervousness in Oddo's voice. 'Thor . . . vald, and Dufnall. And . . . er . . . Kolli the Quiet. We call him that, because he . . . can't speak.'

Dúngal could feel the tension of the others. They all waited for the Captain to jeer, or question them. But he just gestured to a pile of weapons.

'Choose some gear,' he said.

Dúngal dived for a helmet and almost knocked himself out as he dropped it over his head. He teetered, the heavy weight of the iron bending his neck. The helmet was too big and hung down over his eyes, so he could hardly see, and the nosepiece reached to his chin. But he heaved a sigh of relief. His red hair and freckles were hidden.

He peered out at the others. Father Connlae was struggling to untangle the laces of his leather jerkin from his fake beard. Thora's jerkin hung below her knees, but her eyes sparkled with excitement beneath her iron helmet.

'They're coming,' she whispered. 'Here, take a spear.'

There were loud voices and footsteps, and the next moment the rest of the crew crowded around, jostling for weapons.

'Everyone ready?' The Captain's voice rose above the din, then the crowd fell quiet and shuffled apart.

Dúngal realised the four of them had been left standing in a huddle, as the rest formed a circle.

'Come on, you new lads.'

A gap opened for them. When Dúngal moved, he felt as wobbly as if his arms and legs were just a jumble of bare bones, rattling together. Somehow, he stumbled into his place.

Captain Snari began to speak. Dúngal straightened his back, trying to stand steady and proud. His hands holding the spear and shield were sticky with sweat.

'Men, are you ready to swear your loyalty?' asked Snari. His stern eyes travelled around the circle and each person murmured a *yes*. Everyone but Father Connlae. Snari breathed hard and glared at the priest.

'Kolli the Quiet, can you hear me? Are you ready?' he demanded.

'Nod yes,' hissed Dúngal. To his relief, the priest gently lowered his head.

The Captain selected an arrow from his quiver, and fitted it to his bow. Dúngal began to tremble.

'Odin shall have you all!' bellowed Snari.

The arrow flew from his bow and soared over the

circle. Dúngal squeaked and leapt forward as the arrow thudded into the ground behind his heels. The Vikings roared with laughter.

Dúngal's eyes met Oddo's and he felt the other boy's sympathy flow towards him.

'You are now sworn in,' cried Snari. 'Every man here pledges to avenge the others as he would his brothers, and not one of you, no matter how perilous things may be, shall speak a word of fear or dread.'

Dúngal ran his eyes resentfully around the circle of Vikings. 'You're not my brothers,' he muttered. Then his eyes lit on Oddo again. He stared at the thin boy with the heavy iron helmet on his head, the boy who'd despised his curach but come on the voyage in spite of his fears. The boy who'd nearly lost his life, just to help a strange Irish thrall.

'You can be my brother,' whispered Dúngal. 'I make my pledge to you. I will avenge you, no matter how perilous things may be.'

The Captain tugged his arrow from the ground and with a roar of cheering and a rattle of weapons the Vikings raced for the longship. Dúngal turned to take Father Connlae's arm, and saw Oddo on the other side. The three of them hurried towards the ship.

'Wait!' Thora, in the heavy helmet and jerkin, was straggling behind. 'Remember *me*?' she said crossly, as she panted up to join them.

As they drew closer, Dúngal was astounded by *Striker's* size. The prow, carved in the shape of a striking eagle, towered over his head, and when he climbed over the black tarred sides he gaped at the rows of benches stretching from bow to stern. To his dismay, the four friends were separated. Dúngal found himself on a rowing bench beside a sullen man with a dark, weather-beaten face. He peered round worriedly for the priest and spied him a few rows back, sitting in front of Thora.

'Thora, look after him!' he pleaded silently.

'Cast off!' ordered Snari from his raised platform in the stern.

Dúngal's mouth felt dry as the cables were slipped from the mooring posts and the longship pushed away from the bank.

'Raise oars!'

Striker rocked violently as each man stood and with a noisy clatter grabbed an oar from the rack. They lowered their oars over the sides, then sat down ready for action. Dúngal realised the muscles in his back were already tense and aching.

The Captain nodded to the coxswain beneath him.

'Ready-y-y . . . Stroke!' cried the coxswain in a piercing voice.

With all his strength, Dúngal plunged his oar into the water.

'We're not digging for oysters,' snarled the man next to him.

131

Startled, Dúngal heaved up his blade, splattering them both with water. He tried again, this time taking care not to dip so deep.

'Stroke,' called the coxswain. 'Stroke . . . Stroke . . .'

'Keep the beat!' growled the man. '*Listen!*'

Cheeks burning, Dúngal strove to keep time. From the corner of his eye, he could see the oars up and down the boat swinging in unison.

'How long do I have to keep this up for?' wondered Dúngal. His arms and chest were burning with pain. With a feeling of doom, he remembered Father Connlae's shaky hands.

Behind him, there was a *splash* and a cry. The coxswain halted in his chant. The even sweep of blades wavered, then broke into disarray.

'Hold oars!' bellowed the Captain.

Dúngal twisted round and saw the priest, his face aghast, leaning over the side and trying to reach an oar that was floating away. There were rumbles of anger around him.

At that moment, a gust of wind whistled through the longship. There was a loud *snap* from the top of the mast and the pennant streamed outwards, the wings on the black embroidered eagle stretching and flapping. Dúngal saw the Captain glance round in astonishment. A moment before, the weather had been still and calm. Now the wind was lifting cloaks, whipping hair, and sending waves crashing against the ship.

'Hoist sail!' bellowed Snari.

Dúngal glimpsed Father Connlae's look of startled relief as the men tossed their oars on the rack and sprang into action. In a moment, everyone was yelling, grabbing at lines, twisting and tugging. As the yard rattled up the mast, Oddo caught Dúngal's eye, and winked, his face split in an ecstatic, toothy grin. Of course, the wind was Oddo's doing!

Dúngal grinned too, and then a line was thrust into his hand and he was told to make himself useful. The rope snaked through his fingers and the sail started to unfurl. Blue and yellow stripes rippled into view. Dúngal felt his heart thud with excitement.

'I'm going home!' he thought. 'I'm really going home!'

ᛏᛚ ᛒᚱᛇᛟ

23
Unmasked

Oddo's benchmate, a young man named Völund, had muscly arms tanned to the colour of acorns, and blond hair bleached almost white. His eyes, crinkled at the edges from squinting out to sea, were alert and watchful. Several times after Oddo had whispered to the wind, he found those eyes gazing at him quizzically.

All that day and night, Oddo drove *Striker* to the east. The next morning, there were heavy, grey clouds pressing down from a gloomy sky. The water was dark and choppy, and the wind biting. Oddo was glad of his heavy leather jerkin and the iron helmet, but soon his hands were numb with cold. He glanced sideways and saw Völund watching him intently, an amused expression on his face. Oddo hunched his shoulders and huffed on his fingers.

The waves rose higher and the longship heaved and fell in sickening lurches. There was a flash of lightning and a grumble of thunder.

'Storm coming,' warned the Captain. 'Shorten sail!'

As everyone scrambled to their feet, Oddo snatched the opportunity to glance up, and whisper to the clouds. A moment later, the sky was clear, the wind eased, and the sun streamed down. The Captain stared about him, with a bewildered expression on his face. Oddo caught Thora's eye and saw her clap a hand over her mouth to stifle her giggles.

That evening, Völund nudged Oddo and pointed to a spot on the horizon. Oddo could see strange columns of cloud stretching from sea to sky.

'That'll be the Isles of Faer,' said Völund. 'You watch.'

Sure enough, in the morning Oddo was woken by the screeches of thousands of seabirds, and behind the mist of cloud he could make out the black, craggy cliffs of the Isles. He shivered, remembering his last visit here, trapped in a bird shape.

'Land ahoy!' squealed the lookout.

Heads bobbed up between the benches as the men wriggled out of their fur sleeping bags. The carved eagle on the prow seemed to swoop towards the rocks.

'All right, wind, ease off,' hissed Oddo.

Sailors tumbled onto rowing benches, oars in hand, and strove to bring the longship safe to shore.

Oddo glowered at the high, pounding surf. 'Wish I could tell *you* to go away.'

To his astonishment, a huge roller stopped in midair, and slid backwards. *Striker's* hectic reeling changed into a gentle glide. Oddo stared, and everyone on board fell into a stunned silence. The only sound was the *splish splash* of oars, and then the keel grated against the beach. Nobody moved. They sat, gawping at a sea that lay around them as still and unrippling as a puddle.

'What happened?' whispered the Captain.

Beside Oddo, Völund stirred and cleared his throat.

'This boy,' he said, and Oddo felt his belly twist and tighten like a knotted rope, 'he talks to the wind . . . and the waves.'

Everyone on board turned to stare.

'Is this true?' demanded Snari.

Oddo's eyes swept down the long rows of benches and found Thora. She shrugged. He lifted his gaze to the bewildered Captain.

'I . . . Yes . . . I have magic powers,' he croaked.

'He conjured up the wind that brought us here!' called Thora.

'*Well!*' The word was a gush of air, like the blowing of a whale. 'Seems we've got ourselves a perfect crew!'

On shore, everyone set to work filling water kegs and lighting a fire. But when they gathered to watch the huge cauldron bubbling over the flames, Oddo found himself peppered with questions.

136

'What other magic can you do?' one sailor demanded.

'Can you tell my fortune?'

'Can you carve my shield with runes that bring long life?'

'I always thought you looked a bit peculiar', commented a loud voice.

'*Me?!*' Oddo glanced at Thora with her jagged haircut, Father Connlae with his fake beard, and Dúngal with his red hair and freckles. 'If you only knew!' he thought.

Then the food was ready, and everyone turned their attention to the steaming bowls of oatmeal.

Oddo and his companions slipped away to a grassy slope out of sight of the crowd. They were relieved to escape for a short time from the worry of pretence. Oddo lay back, luxuriating in the feel of warm sun on aching muscles. He brushed the hair from his eyes.

'That's what Arni does,' said Thora.

'What?'

'Pushes his hair up like that.'

'Well, he's always got a long fringe.'

'Yes, but . . . you look so much like him.'

'Well, I thought you looked like my mother the other day.'

'You *did*?' Thora sat up. 'Why?'

'Oh, I don't know, you've both got round faces or something.'

'Isn't it strange,' said Thora, 'all my family are long and thin like you, and I've got chubby cheeks like Sigrid.'

'It's as if you're in the wrong families,' chuckled Dúngal.

Oddo and Thora didn't laugh. They stared at each other.

'We were born on the same night,' said Thora in a small voice.

'You don't think . . . Gyda the Midwife mixed us up?'

'It would explain why you can do magic and I can't!'

'It couldn't happen . . . Two babies in different houses . . .'

'I know, but . . . I'm going to ask Gyda when we see her!'

It seemed to Oddo as if his life and Thora's had smashed together, and shattered like two clay pots. And now the fragments were whirling around in his head. He kept seeing his own face, and Thora's. He heard his mother's words, 'Just like a daughter,' and his father, in a temper, 'I can't believe I fathered such a weakling.' And from the dazed look in Thora's eyes, he could see that she felt the same.

When it was time to board again, the men were buzzing with excitement. Their voices had a light-hearted ring and they all clapped him on the back as they passed. Even Captain Snari was chortling and rubbing his hands.

'We'll row clear of the islands,' he said, 'then, Oddo, you can conjure the wind up for us, and we'll hoist sail.'

Oddo snapped back to the present. He glanced up

at the sails. 'We want to go south now, don't we?' he asked. He frowned at the sky. The midday sun gave him little clue which direction was which. He bent towards Hairydog, whose nose was poking out beneath the rowing bench. 'Hey,' he whispered, 'come out and have a scratch.'

The dog wriggled out and began to scratch vigorously with her hind leg. Oddo squatted next to her and peered at the tiny fleas that dropped from her back and hopped around the deck. From the corner of his eye, he saw Völund watching in bewilderment.

Oddo took his seat again.

'What were you *doing*?' asked Völund.

Oddo grinned. 'Just looking which way to go.' He pointed south, and called the wind.

'But . . .? How?' Völund stared at the deck, then up to the sky.

'Raise oars!' bellowed the Captain.

As the oars clattered around them, Oddo relented. 'It's the fleas,' he explained. 'They show me where to go. They always hop north!'

The wind picked up, and they headed for Ireland. But as they sailed on their way, Oddo was still wondering about the night he was born.

ᛋᚠ ᚹᛖᛚᚦ...

24
A gift for the King

Dúngal gazed down the rows of benches. While Oddo kept the longship on a steady course, the crewmen lounged, clicking the little wooden pieces on their board games, or tilting their drinking horns. Even the steersman had tied up his steering oar and was joining in.

Thora sidled up to Dúngal. 'We're nearly there,' she whispered. 'If we can make it through just a few more hours with no one noticing our disguises, we'll be safe.'

Dúngal nodded. He turned back to watch the coast, straining his eyes for the rocky finger of Benn Étair which beckoned wanderers home to Ériu. At last he saw it, a tall crag, standing alone on a long, sandy spit.

'There it is!' yelled a voice behind him. 'We've reached Dyflinn!'

'Dyflinn?' muttered Dúngal. 'It's called *Dublinn*, you ignorant Viking.'

As they entered the bay, he gazed across the silver-blue water to the perfect rolling hills. Somewhere, behind those green slopes, he would find his kinsfolk again. He turned and looked the length of the ship to Oddo, standing proud beside the Captain. Their eyes met.

'Thank you,' whispered Dúngal, though Oddo couldn't hear.

The sail came down and they rowed up the River Liffey towards the centre of town. The market hove into sight and when Dúngal saw the rows of slaves, bound in iron, his hands tightened on the oar.

They passed the earthen ramparts that protected the fortress of King Yvar the Viking. They swung into the pool of dark water, stained brown by the peat bog, which gave the town its name: Dub Linn – dark pool.

Their journey was ended.

As Dúngal stumbled off the ship onto the wooden dock, Thora rushed to his side.

'We made it! We're safe!' she hissed.

Dúngal grinned back. 'And wasn't I telling you I'd get back to Ériu?' he retorted.

Yapping excitedly, Hairydog bounded over the side of the ship. A moment later Oddo and Father Connlae joined them.

'This can't be Ireland,' said Oddo. 'It looks like a Viking town!'

'It is a Viking town,' growled Dúngal. 'On Irish soil. They've even put in a Viking king! Those marauders use Dublinn as their raiding base for the rest of Ireland.' He scowled at all the longships clustered in the pool, at the Viking encampment, and the huge bulk of the King's fortress. 'Tíagam ass. Let's get out of here!'

As they turned to go, Captain Snari let out a yell.

'Hey! You!' Feet pounded towards them. 'Where do you think you're going?'

The four of them hesitated, glancing at each other. Dúngal felt a warning surge of fear. He saw Father Connlae's pale, shocked face, and the wisps of hair hanging from his chin, and knew they were about to be unmasked.

'Run!' he cried.

He leapt forward, thinking for a fleeting instant they might escape. But it was too late. The crew closed in. They were surrounded by a palisade of spears.

Snari stepped through, and glared down at them. 'What do you think you're up to?' he demanded. 'You swore allegiance to my ship! You don't go traipsing off till I give you permission!'

Dúngal gaped at him. This pompous oaf was only worried about losing his crew. He hadn't seen through their disguise at all!

'As it happens,' continued Snari, 'we'll be in dock for a while, so you may amuse yourselves for a few hours. Except for that Oddo boy. He's too valuable to go wandering. Völund, Egil, bring him to me! I intend to present him as a gift to King Yvar!'

Dúngal saw Oddo stiffen in shock.

'You can't give me away!' he protested. 'I'm not a thrall! I'm a Viking!'

The Captain snorted. 'I can do what I like,' he said. 'I'm your Captain.'

The two tallest sailors took hold of Oddo's arms.

'No!'

Oddo tried to twist free, and Hairydog leapt forward with a snarl. Two spears clanged in front of her nose.

'Like this in your ribs?' growled a crewman.

'Thora . . . Thorvald, look after Hairydog!' cried Oddo.

They had a glimpse of his white, terrified face.

'This can't be happening!' thought Dúngal. 'Oddo was the only safe one!' He glanced at Thora clutching Hairydog, at the priest blinking in bemusement. 'We can't just stand here. Even Hairydog did more than that!'

Clenching his fists, he stepped forward.

'Dúnga-al!' Thora's voice was urgent and warning, but there was a pounding in Dúngal's head.

'I'm the thrall,' he yelled. 'You blind, stupid Vikings, can't you *see*? I'm Irish. Look at me!' He flung off his helmet and hurled himself at the astonished captors. '*I'm* the one to take, you brainless heaps of dung!'

ᚴ

25
Prisoners

'Dúngal, what on earth made you do it?' Oddo demanded.

They were both huddled on the floor of a tiny, stone-walled room. Dúngal pressed his head against his knees.

'You're my friend,' he mumbled. 'And . . . I swore the Viking oath. To be your brother without fear or dread.'

Oddo looked at the bowed head and sighed.

'So now we're both in trouble.'

Regretfully, he fingered the goatskin tied around his shoulders. If he'd been on his own, he could have drawn it up over his head, turned invisible, and escaped.

There was a crunch of feet on the gravel outside.

The bolt slid back and the door opened. Oddo shielded his eyes against the glare of daylight flooding the room. Broad-shouldered Egil stood in the doorway.

'Come on, boys,' he said. 'On your feet. You're going to meet the King!'

The two of them got up stiffly and followed Egil across the yard and into the street.

'Look!' whispered Dúngal.

'Where?'

Up and down the winding street, there were crowds of bustling people, and the tiny houses and workshops lining the roadway seemed to press forward, the weavers, carvers, blacksmiths and leatherworkers spilling outwards.

Oddo heard a stifled bark and saw, in the shadow of an oak tree, a dog and two watching figures.

'Thora and Hairydog and Father Connlae!' he breathed. As he and Dúngal were hustled down the street, he sensed the others leaving the shadows to follow behind. He cast a glance over his shoulder, and tried to smile.

The rampart of the King's fortress rose before them. The high bank of earth was topped by a palisade of hazel and blackthorn, and guarded by wooden watch-towers. Many eyes in iron helmets watched them approach. They rounded the wall and saw Captain Snari waiting beside the entrance. He rubbed his hands and beamed.

'Ready to meet the King?'

Oddo saw Dúngal's eyes dart about, as if he was looking for a way to escape. But the Captain kept a firm grip on their arms, and when the guards opened the wooden gates, they were hustled down the long tunnel into the fortress.

Inside, there was a scatter of buildings, small and thatched, like the ones in the street. Snari marched them past a blacksmith hammering at an anvil, a potter slapping his clay, a milking shed, a pigsty, and up to the longhouse in the centre. Hangings of exotic yellow fur, dappled with rings of black, covered the doorway. A guard swept the draperies aside and, prodded by the Captain, Oddo and Dúngal stepped forward.

The vast hall shimmered with colours, lights and sound. Music poured from the fingers of a man who crouched on a cushion, his pointed fingernails rippling across the brass strings of the instrument he held to his shoulder. All around the room, scores of oil lamps flickered and glowed. Steaming copper pots glinted above the leaping flames in the central hearth. Richly clad people feasted at a long table that stretched all the way along the wide platform at the side of the room. The white tablecloth was almost hidden under the dishes and spillages of their meal. Coloured tapestries hung on the wall behind them, and high carved seat pillars marked the place of honour. Oddo's eyes were drawn to the man seated between the pillars.

'That must be the King,' he whispered.

The man had a fringe of dark hair hanging over eyes that were sunk deep in a gaunt face. A black beard reached halfway down his chest. His plum-coloured cloak was embroidered with silver and pinned with a huge gold clasp. In place of a drinking horn, he held a jewelled goblet and when he tilted it, a gold ring glinted on his finger.

'Come.' Captain Snari sounded nervous as he tugged the boys towards the table.

A skald performing for the guests ended his ballad, and the people seated along the table cheered and clapped. Serving girls hurried forward, bringing more courses for the banquet – shining haunches of pork, whole roasted birds, and strange dishes fragrant with herbs and spices. Oddo gave a longing sniff.

'Why am I always hungry?' he thought.

The applause faded, and the Captain seized his chance.

'Your Majesty!' he called.

The King was tearing strips off a long, meaty bone with his teeth, but he raised his eyebrows enquiringly.

'Your Majesty, I am Captain Snari of the longship *Striker*. I have travelled from the new settlement in Iceland to trade here. I have great pleasure in presenting you with a gift as a gesture of my loyalty. This is Oddo the Wind Master – a boy with magic powers! And,' he jerked his head at Dúngal, 'his humble companion.'

The King chewed in silence, his eyes on the two captives. When the bone was picked clean, he lifted the tablecloth to wipe his beard, toppling drinks and scattering dishes.

'What magic powers?' he demanded.

'Why . . . he can command the wind and the waves!'

'You ignorant fool,' snapped the King. 'I can do that myself. It is a simple matter for a king to bend the weather to his will!'

Face flaming with embarrassment, Captain Snari began to back out of the room.

'I can speak to birds, I can read the runes!' King Yvar continued.

'Then please . . .' Snari paused and spread out his arms. 'Please keep them as your thralls. They can harvest your corn and milk your cows. They will make good thralls. They are strong, young . . .' He was still speaking as he slipped from the room.

Thralls? Oddo gaped in disbelief as the draperies swung back over an empty doorway.

ᚾᛁᚱ ᛁᛋ ᚨ ᚱᚢᛏ

26
The black horse

Thora gave a shaky smile as Father Connlae handed her a bowl of gruel. They were seated at a table in a crowded room, and the kind family who'd given them shelter was plying them with food. As Thora lifted the bowl to her lips, her eyes fell on Hairydog. The dog's meal was untouched and she was poised in the doorway, watching Thora reproachfully.

Thora glanced at Father Connlae. He was smiling while he sipped, his pale eyes fixed dreamily on the toddler of the family. The child with gruel dripping down his chin made Thora think of her own scruffy little brother.

'Ketil,' she moaned. 'If only I could get back to you!'

Surrounded by this crowd of strangers, she felt more

lonely than she'd ever felt in her life. She was haunted by the image of her two best friends disappearing down the tunnel to the fortress. She stumbled to her feet, her eyes blurred with tears, and made for the door. A chorus of Irish gibberish followed her, but she just nodded and slipped outside.

In the street, she pulled up her hood to hide her face. There were Vikings all around, shouting and laughing, and any one of them might be a sailor from *Striker*, hunting for the runaway crew. Thora was terrified they would catch her and drag her back to the ship.

'Hairydog, heel!' she whispered urgently.

The streets were narrow and crowded, the buildings jammed together, with hardly space for a goat to slip between. Wilting, dusty vegetables were the only plants among the hard paving stones and fences. The air was thick with smoke and the stink of latrines.

Bumped and jostled by the crowds, Thora tried to make her way towards the fortress.

'We've got to find a way to rescue the boys,' she told Hairydog. But they soon found themselves gathered up by the throng, and swept into the market.

There was a bonfire blazing in the middle of the square, a festive buzz among the booths, and everywhere, freckled noses and red hair just like Dúngal's. Irish girls tossed their russet locks as they danced around the fire, while a piper whistled on his bone flute. Youths snatched handfuls of bilberries from overflowing baskets, staining their grinning faces with indigo juice. They scuffled for the attention of the girls, overbalancing mounds of fat, round cabbages, and sending sticky honeycombs tumbling from the stands.

Older women were busy wrangling with the vendors, and piling their baskets with wild garlic, bunches of watercress, bread, berries and cabbages. But to Thora's puzzlement, the most popular wares were rowan branches. The green boughs, with their clusters of bright red berries, dangled from every basket.

'What do you want with those?' she asked, but everyone just shook their heads and turned away.

Thora felt scared and helpless as she realised none of this boisterous mob would understand a word she said, even if she yelled at the top of her voice.

'Dúngal must have felt like this,' she thought, 'when he was captured by the raiders.'

She could feel the chill of evening creeping over the town as she left the market. The crowds were thinning quickly now; everyone seemed anxious to get home. As she and Hairydog hurried along, Thora noticed rowan branches draped above all the doorways.

'Hairydog, wait!'

She stopped and watched as a woman appeared at one door and bent to lay a loaf of bread and a dish of berries on the paving stones outside. Thora swept her eyes along the street and saw that at every house people were doing the same.

'It looks as if they're putting out food for the Little Folk!' she thought. 'What did Dúngal call them? The shee-something. And the rowan branches – at home we hang them up for protection from evil magic. Could it be the same here?'

She was beginning to feel frightened. The streets were almost deserted, and half the houses lay in pools of darkness. Everyone seemed to be hiding inside their homes. Only the Viking raiders still loitered, their loud voices piercing the dusk.

'Hairydog, what's happening?' whispered Thora.

The dog growled and all the hairs on her neck bristled. Thora heard a soft ripple of song, and something gentle as a cat's tail brushed about her ankles. She looked down. Streaming across the paving stones, transparent as water, were the figures of tiny people. Little Folk!

Thora felt as if her hair, like Hairydog's, was standing on end.

There was the *cloppety clop* of a horse cantering down the street behind her. Hairydog took off faster than an arrow from a bow, and to Thora's astonishment, Vikings began to race past her, yelling in fright. She heard the horse slow to a halt. It let out a whinny and she felt its breath blast through her cloak, hot as fire. She swung round.

The beast was black as a moonless night but when it tossed its head, she saw flames where there should have been eyes, and from its nostrils there were streams of smoke and fire. It whinnied again, and reared up. As the giant hooves flailed above her head, Thora threw herself backwards. The hooves crashed down where she'd stood, splintering the paving stones, spraying her with gravel. Thora clambered to her feet, and fled.

Down the empty, twisting streets, blind in the darkness, she pounded. And then, bursting out of a narrow alley, she heard the sound of running water, and almost skidded into the river.

She collapsed on the soft earth, and buried her face in the sweet-smelling grass. She listened, every muscle tensed, for the thudding of that monstrous beast; but the only sounds were the gurgle of water and her own sobbing gasps. Gradually she relaxed. She took in a long breath and smelled the scent of camomile. She sat up and looked at the crushed leaves and petals lying in her palm. In the pale moonlight she could see a yellow-centred flower, half torn from its downy grey stem. She smiled, pressed the flower against her nose, and breathed in the sweet apple perfume.

'Camomile to calm the nerves!' she muttered.

Shakily, she rose to her feet. With sinking heart, she realised she had no idea how to find her way to the little cottage where she'd left Father Connlae. And what about Hairydog?

She gazed along the riverbank hoping to catch a glimpse of those perky ears and bushy tail; but her eyes fell instead on the black forbidding bulk of the King's fort.

'If only the horse would go in there,' she thought. 'It would scare away the guards, and Oddo and Dúngal could escape!'

At that moment, she heard a terrified yelping. Hairydog raced out of the alley and plunged towards her. They both toppled to the ground.

'Hairydog!' sobbed Thora with relief, cradling the trembling animal in her arms. 'Here.' She held the camomile to the dog's nose, but Hairydog opened her mouth and snapped it down. 'Hey, you were supposed to smell it.' Thora started to laugh, but then she heard, heading towards them, the thud of hooves. She leapt to her feet. '*Run!*'

She glanced at Hairydog, and was astounded to see her lolling on the bank.

'Hairydog? Can't you hear?'

The dog eyed her and went on calmly chewing the camomile.

Thora stared back. Suddenly a wild, impossible idea began to form in her mind. She threw herself on her knees and tore plants out of the ground, sniffing them frantically. When the black horse trotted out of the alley, Thora was waiting, her heart pounding, her hands filled with flowers.

ᛏᚱ ᛗᚨᚲ ᛋᚱ

27
Lugnasad

Oddo was woken by the sounds of yells and thuds. He peered over the side of the pigsty, where he'd been sleeping. Beside him, Dúngal rolled over and squelched in a heap of dung.

'What's happening?' he groaned.

Oddo squinted into the gloom. Over the cries of alarm, he could hear something heavy smashing against the gate of the fort.

'I think someone's trying to break in,' he said.

The next moment a scattering of guards came flying past and dived into the longhouse. Behind them, thundering out of the darkness, galloped a black giant of a horse. Oddo goggled at the flames that shot from its eye sockets, and the smoke pouring from its nostrils.

Then he lifted his gaze and saw a girl astride the gleaming, quivering flanks, her hands twisted through the long black mane.

'*Thora?!*'

'Oddo! Dúngal!'

The horse slowed to a halt. There was a *yip* and Hairydog erupted out of the darkness. She threw herself at the wall of the sty, her tail wagging frantically.

'Thora, what on earth . . .?'

Oddo hurdled the wall, then stepped back hastily as the black horse stamped and snorted. To his astonishment, Thora calmly patted its neck, then reached for a knotted corner of her cloak. She drew out a flower, leaned forward, and popped it between the horse's gnashing teeth. The creature gave a soft whinny and lowered its head to chew.

'Quick!' called Thora. 'Climb up.'

'No!' Dúngal clutched Oddo's arm. 'It's the horse of the Sídaigi. Look!'

He pointed downwards with a shaking finger. The ground was rippling as if it were covered with waves. There were a myriad tiny figures, hardly more solid than shadows, running across the surface.

'What are they?' whispered Oddo.

'The Sídaigi. The Little Folk. If we can see them, then tonight must be Lugnasad – one of the nights when they cross over from the Other World.'

'Come on!' cried Thora. 'Hurry up, before the guards come back.'

Oddo tried to step towards her, but Dúngal held him in a fierce grip.

'You mustn't,' he said. 'The Sídaigi will be furious.'

'Why?'

'Because that's *their* horse!' he exploded. 'Their *magic* horse. I don't know how Thora's managed to ride it, but they won't be happy. And we haven't put out food or gifts for them or anything. We don't even have rowan branches for protection.'

'Bursting blueberries,' yelled Thora. 'Don't you two want to escape?'

She slid off the horse's back, and Oddo watched, fascinated, as the Sídaigi parted and streamed around her feet like a river round a rock. The next instant, he heard the squeals of piglets in the sty, and spinning round he saw the Sídaigi tugging at their curly tails. The same moment, there was a frightened lowing from the byre, and startled squawks from the hen roosts.

It was then he felt the first tickling at his ankles. He looked down and saw the Sídaigi swarming over his feet. In seconds, he could feel thousands of tiny fingers and toes crawling up his body, tugging and pinching, all the way up to the top of his head. He hopped and squirmed, attempting to brush them away, but they clung as tight as limpets to a rock. When he grabbed them and tried to pull them off, they wound themselves in his hair. Hairydog whirled around, yelping and snapping at her tiny tormentors. Dúngal bellowed in Irish.

'How do we get rid of them?' cried Oddo.

'I think,' panted Dúngal, 'they follow their horse.' He let out a few more Irish curses. 'We've got to get rid of that beast!'

'But I brought it so you could run away!' wailed Thora.

'Then take it back again!'

At that moment, Oddo managed to wrench one of the Sídaigi out of his hair. He stared at it writhing on his palm, and then it disappeared. He felt a trickling sensation running from the top of his head, and realised it was the other Sídaigi pouring downwards. For a second, the ground was covered again with the tiny running figures, then they seemed to melt and vanish into the earth, like snow under the warmth of the sun.

'They've gone!' he croaked.

He turned slowly on his heel. Even the black horse had vanished. And in the east, a tiny finger of light was showing in the sky.

'It's dawn,' breathed Dúngal. 'Lugnasad's over!'

At that moment, there were bellows of rage from the longhouse. The guards burst out again, looking sheepish, and headed back to the gate. All around the fort, other figures began to creep outdoors. They peered around, and broke into excited chatter.

Oddo turned to look at Thora. She was drooping now with disappointment, and he wanted to fling out his arms and hug her tight. But when she sensed him looking at her, she gave a wobbly smile and shrugged her shoulders.

'Well,' she said, 'at least we're all together again. Now what are we going to do?'

ᚲᛁᛗᛒᛖᛘᚱ...

28
A bargain with the King

Oddo dragged the rake through the hay, sweeping it into a neat pile. Up and down the field, other thralls were doing the same, and the hot summer air was filled with swirls of dust and the scent of hay. Beside him, Thora sneezed for the hundredth time. She sniffed and wiped her hand across the reddened tip of her nose.

'Hey you, don't slack!' A burly overseer prodded her with his stick, as if she was a cow or a horse.

Oddo ground his teeth.

'Oddo! Oddo the Wind Master!'

Oddo jerked his head round in surprise. A guard, his hands cupped around his mouth, was calling from the edge of the field.

Dúngal grabbed the rake from Oddo's hand and threw it on the pile of hay.

'Come on, let's see what he wants!'

Oddo shot a worried glance at Thora, struggling with her heavy rake, then he followed Dúngal towards the yelling guard.

'What is it?' Oddo demanded.

The man's brows shot upwards, and his voice rose with surprise. 'You're the Wind Master?' Oddo nodded.

'Then the King requests the favour of an audience,' pronounced the guard.

As the boys entered the longhouse, the King swung round and glared at Oddo from his deep-sunk eyes.

'So, Oddo the Wind Master, you have stopped my cows from giving milk and my fowls from laying eggs. You have terrified my steeds and put my swine off their food!'

'I . . . It wasn't . . .' Oddo started to speak, but Dúngal jabbed him in the ribs.

'It seems you can do more than just command the weather!' continued the King. 'I was too hasty in my judgement, and you have taken your revenge. If I now offer you reward, will you lift the enchantment?'

'What reward?' Dúngal demanded before Oddo had a chance to answer.

The King raised his eyebrows. 'You may have your freedom,' he announced. 'Tomorrow, if all is well, you shall both be free to leave this fort.'

He waved imperiously and the boys backed out of the room. Oddo grabbed his friend by the arm.

'What did you say that for?' he hissed. 'You know it wasn't me who upset the animals. It was the Sídaigi!'

'So what? It got you what you wanted.'

'Are you crazy? Now I have to lift the spells! How'm I supposed to do that?!'

Dúngal chortled.

'That's the joke,' he said. 'Lugnasad's over, remember? The Sídaigi have left, so the spells will go away anyway! Tomorrow, everything will be back to normal. The cows'll give milk, the hens'll lay eggs. Everyone will be happy. We'll get out of this place, and I'll go home!'

That night they were invited to a banquet in the longhouse. Afterwards, Oddo was offered a fine carved bed, and Dúngal was shown to a place on the floor beside the fire. They looked at each other. Thora and Hairydog would be waiting for them by the pigsty.

'I . . . we . . . have to go outside. To lift the enchantment,' mumbled Oddo.

Hairydog saw them coming, and barked a welcome.

'What happened? What did old Yvar want?' demanded Thora as they flopped beside her.

'In a minute,' panted Oddo. 'First, now no one's listening, tell us how you tamed that horse.'

Thora grinned. 'Just used herbs,' she said.

Oddo gazed at her and shook his head. 'I don't know how you dared to go so close,' he said. 'And . . . to *ride* it!'

'I did it so I could rescue you,' said Thora, and then she made a face. 'I didn't know the Sídaigi were going to follow me.'

'Where the black horse goes, the Sídaigi follow,' Dúngal intoned. Then he burst out laughing. 'Lucky they did,' he spluttered. 'You got the King really scared!'

'You should have seen Dúngal!' said Oddo. 'He bossed the King!'

Between chuckles and exclamations, they told Thora about Dúngal's demand, and the King's promise.

Then the three of them snuggled down together, and closed their eyes.

Around them, the fort settled for the night. Chimney smoke dwindled away. Voices dropped to a murmur and fell silent. The only sounds were the occasional whiffle of a horse in the stable, and the grunt of the sow in the sty.

The sun sank below the horizon.

'*Clu-u-uck, clu-u-uck!*' The peace was shattered by the terrified screeches of hens. Tumbling from their perches, wings flapping, they scuttered across the yard. A volley of whinnies rang out from the stables. Hooves hammered in panic against the wooden doors. At the same moment, cows started to bellow in the barn, the piglets squealed in the pigsty, and all around the enclosure dogs began to yelp with fright.

Oddo grabbed Dúngal and thrust his face close to the small, freckled nose.

'You said the Sídaigi would be gone!' he shouted.

Dúngal shoved Oddo away.

'It can't be the Sídaigi,' he said. 'Look!' He spun round, pointing wildly. 'See, there aren't any!'

'They must be invisible, you stupid half-witted peabrain!' Oddo clutched his hair. '*Listen* to them!' He gazed at Dúngal in despair. 'Just because they only *show* themselves on – Luny night or whatever you call it, doesn't mean they just . . . Obviously, if they're annoyed enough, they come back again!'

'*Annoyed?* They'd be spitting bones! Your idiot Vikings didn't even leave one gift for them.'

Human shouts were added to the squeals and growls, as figures erupted from the buildings around them. The flames of their torches bobbed and wavered.

'What's going on? What's happening?' they shouted.

Oddo flopped down and buried his face in his hands.

'What's the King going to say now?' he moaned.

'I've still got some camomile,' cried Thora. She dived over the wall of the sty, and pulled out the knotted woollen square she'd bundled behind the feed trough. 'Find that black horse, and I'll take it away!'

'*I'll* find it!' said Dúngal, and raced into the shadows.

Oddo looked at Thora. 'If we can't see the Sídaigi, we won't be able to see their horse,' he said.

'But you're magic. You *must* be able to see them!'

Oddo shook his head. At that moment there came a *thud* behind them, as of a spear banging the ground. Oddo saw Thora's eyes widen. He spun round.

'You have made your point,' said the voice of King Yvar. His face loured, shadowed and craggy, in the light cast by the guards' torches. His long, bony fingers combed through his beard, then twisted and let go. 'I see I must offer a better reward to persuade you to lift the enchantment.' He reached out and fastidiously lifted a corner of Oddo's cloak. 'Perhaps new garments,' he said. 'Yours are not fit for one of your status. Throw this rag on the dung heap and permit me to offer you my own cloak instead. It is woven from silk spun in the Lands of the East.'

'No!' Oddo clutched the goatskin and stepped back.

From the other side he felt Thora grab the cloak too. 'Oddo, this is the goatskin!'

He turned to look at her. 'So?'

'*So?!*' She leaned forward to hiss in his ear. 'Make yourself invisible, then maybe you'll be able to see *other* invisible things.'

Oddo stared, then glanced back at the King. He was still speaking pompously.

'. . . a ship,' he was saying, 'loaded with any cargo you desire – barrels of wheat, bales of wool, silver . . . gold . . .'

He paused, waiting for an answer.

Oddo just looked at him, then took hold of the goatskin and lifted it over his head.

<

29
Hurry!

King Yvar and the guards backed away, goggling like three stranded fish. Thora grinned with satisfaction as they disappeared into the longhouse.

The next moment, Dúngal pounded up to her.

'I can't find it,' he panted. 'I saw a black horse in a stable, but it wasn't the right one.' He paused, and looked around. 'Where's Oddo?'

Thora chuckled. 'He's turned invisible,' she said. 'He's looking for the Sídaigi.'

'I'm still here, you know,' said Oddo's voice.

Dúngal and Thora squealed excitedly.

'Well, can you see them?' demanded Thora.

There was a pause. She felt Dúngal grip her arm.

'I think I can,' said Oddo. 'Just . . . faint . . . glimpses.'

His voice faded as he moved away.

'Find the horse,' called Thora.

They waited, hardly breathing. A guard came past, shoving them roughly out of his path. Then the torches and human shouts died away.

'They're all hiding inside,' said Thora.

'They're scared,' smirked Dúngal.

'I wish Oddo would hurry!'

The piglets were squealing at the tops of their voices. Thora glanced down at Hairydog. She was cowering on the ground, whimpering.

'It's all right, Hairydog. Oddo's going to save us.'

Thora bent to stroke the dog's back, and thought she felt tiny feet scamper across her hand. She shuddered, and hastily stood up again.

There was the sound of running, then Oddo burst into view in front of them, pulling off his hood, and gasping for breath.

'It's coming,' he panted. 'Quick, Thora, your herbs!'

'But . . . I can't see it . . . It'll stamp on me, crush me! I thought you . . .'

Oddo swung away from her and pulled the goatskin up again.

'*I* don't know what to do!' he cried. 'Hurry!'

Thora could feel the ground vibrating as the beast charged towards them. She snatched up her bundle and began tearing at the knot.

'I can't undo it!'

'Hurry!'

She gripped it with her teeth and wrenched hard. The fabric ripped, and Dúngal dived to catch the flowers as they tumbled downwards.

'Here.' He thrust them towards her. She could feel his hand shaking as their fingers touched.

There was a *thud, thud, thud* as if the creature was pawing the ground. Then the sound stopped, and Thora knew the horse was rearing up, its huge hooves flailing above her head. She started to back away, but the wall of the sty was pressing against her legs. She thrust out her hand, the flowers with their yellow centres and white petals nestled on her palm. The ground seemed to explode in front of her. Searing heat streamed towards her.

Then the flowers vanished.

'Quick!' Thora reached up, felt the massive neck, bulging with muscle, and ran her hand along the heaving flank. 'Give me a leg-up. Hurry, I don't have any more flowers!'

'*What?!*'

'*Hurry!*'

She grasped the mane, and hauled herself up over the huge, invisible mass. Her leg was half over the monster's back when she felt it rear. She flew into the air, her arms almost ripped from their sockets. Then she crashed down, every bone in her body rattling, as the creature dropped back to earth.

'Let go!' cried Oddo. 'Get off!'

'No!' she screamed.

'You'll be killed!'

But Thora was astride now, wild with triumph. She lifted her heels and kicked, hard as she could, at the horse's flanks. She felt as if her feet were bashing into a wall of iron, but a tremor ran through the creature's body, and the next moment, it was plunging forward. She felt the flames from its eyeholes stream backwards, burning her cheek, singeing her hair. She could hear Hairydog racing behind them, yipping with excitement.

They sped past the longhouse, scattering a woodpile and smashing through a haystack. Thora shook the hay from her eyes, then saw the wooden gate loom ahead. She had a glimpse of tree trunks strapped across broken palings. Then she felt the muscles gather under her, and the massive horse launched itself at the gate. It hit with an impact that tore Thora's hands from their grasp, and she screamed as she found herself flying into the air.

ᚾᛁᛈ ᚻᛁᛋ ᚱᛁᚾ

30
Treasure

'I can't see them any more,' said Oddo, as the last flicker of the fireball eyes faded into the distance. For an instant he could still hear the thudding of hooves, and Hairydog's frantic barks, then they too were gone.

'And the Sídaigi?' demanded Dúngal.

Oddo looked at the ground and saw a ripple, like a wave receding from a beach. It was the Little Folk pouring after the horse.

'They're leaving,' he said.

There was a pause.

'The piglets have stopped squealing,' said Dúngal.

Oddo listened. There was no more stamping or howling, either. The bellowing and bleating trickled to a stop. The hens gave a last rustle and squawk, and settled on their perches.

Oddo heaved a sigh and pulled off his hood.

'This time they've really gone,' said Dúngal.

'Yes,' said Oddo, but he wasn't thinking of the Sídaigi. He gazed round the dark, peaceful fort. Without Thora, it felt very, very empty.

'Now we can claim the reward,' said Dúngal.

Oddo looked at him but neither of them smiled. They were both picturing a girl hurtling into the darkness on the back of an invisible monster.

'She came here to rescue us,' whispered Oddo. 'And she has.'

He bent to scoop up her cloak, torn and trampled into the earth. A single camomile flower slid out and tumbled to the ground. He stared at it, his eyes blurring with tears.

'There was one more flower,' he whispered.

When the guards shook his shoulder a few hours later, Oddo was asleep against the pigsty, Thora's clothing hugged to his chest. He rose stiffly, and kicked Dúngal awake.

'The King wants to see us,' he mumbled.

In the longhouse, all the lamps were blazing, and on the white-clothed table golden platters glittered with jewels. The King rose to his feet and regarded them, stroking his long black beard.

'Well?' he demanded.

'The spell is lifted,' said Oddo wearily. 'You will have your eggs and milk again.'

'Ah.' King Yvar's mouth twitched. 'Then please . . . Eat!' He gestured to the table.

Oddo and Dúngal sank onto the wooden bench and instantly thralls were flittering around, piling their plates with food.

'Perhaps someone else could look after your . . . ah . . . belongings,' said King Yvar.

Oddo started, and realised he was still clutching Thora's ragged bundle. He laid it beside him, picked up a piece of the fine wheat bread, and took a bite.

'When you are ready,' continued the King, 'we will adjourn to the river and you will select your ship.'

Oddo looked at the uneaten piles of delectables, then glanced at Dúngal. In unison, they gulped their half-chewed mouthfuls, and rose to their feet.

'We'll go now!' said Oddo. The sooner they got out of this fort, the sooner they'd find out what had happened to Thora.

In a few minutes they were seated in the royal long-ship with oarsmen in scarlet and gold rowing them round the bend in the river. Once again, the cluster of longships in the Black Pool hove into sight.

'Choose one that's not too big,' whispered Dúngal. 'We don't have a crew.'

Oddo nodded.

They glided slowly between the wide-bellied cargo ships, and the leering prows of the battle ships. Oddo pointed to the shortest, tubbiest vessel. The furled sail was a cheerful red-and-white stripe.

'That one!' he said.

The King's mouth curled superciliously.

'The hold shall be filled with furs and wines, oil and gold,' he declared.

'As quickly as you can, please,' said Oddo.

'It shall be done.'

'We'll board now,' added Oddo. 'And set sail as soon as it's ready.'

'Do you require a crew?'

Oddo shook his head.

The King's face broke into a broad smile.

'Of course not. You can command the wind and the waves,' he chuckled. 'With this small vessel, you two will manage on your own, hey?'

Oddo drummed his fingers impatiently as the goods were passed down the chain of burly servants and heaved aboard.

'Look at this stuff!' said Dúngal.

He took hold of a butter-coloured fur and draped it around his shoulders. Then he held up a gold platter and waggled it so that the gleaming surfaces flashed in the sunlight. But Oddo was watching the last jar of seal oil being squeezed into the hold.

'That's it!' he cried. 'Hoist sail!'

He glanced at the sky and pointed eagerly down the river, calling the wind. The red and white stripes billowed outwards, and the little cargo ship began to skim across the water.

'When we get around the bend, we'll moor her, and go look for Thora!' called Oddo.

'And Father Connlae!' said Dúngal.

Oddo blinked. He'd almost forgotten the priest.

As they swept past the high walls of the fort, the slave market came into view. Both boys fell silent, looking at the miserable rows of men, women and children, standing in chains. From the corner of his eye, Oddo saw Dúngal's jaw trembling.

'Wait!' cried Oddo. 'Pull up.' He leapt on shore and held out his hand. 'Pass me some of that cargo,' he said. 'We're going to buy every one of those thralls!'

In a few minutes there was pandemonium. The captives laughed and cried and cheered as one by one Oddo set them free. Then they vanished down the maze of streets, and the Viking traders were left gazing in bewilderment at their empty market. One of the traders was Captain Snari. He glared suspiciously at Oddo.

'How did you get all those riches?'

'Just a reward,' said Oddo smugly. 'For my magic.' Snari scowled. 'Ah well, better get back to my ship,' said Oddo.

But as he turned to go, he saw a flash of movement

in a shadowed alley. An arm reached out to beckon him. He hesitated, then sidled towards it, his heart pounding. With a flood of disappointment he saw Father Connlae emerge, alone, from the shadows.

Then, in the distance, he heard a muffled bark.

Oddo began to run, his feet flying over the cobble-stones. As he passed the priest, his eyes raked the alley. There was another bark. Hairydog scampered into sight. And following behind was someone with short, honey-coloured hair and a huge, proud grin.

'You made it!' she shouted. 'You got out!'

Oddo felt tears pouring down his cheeks as he ran towards her. He was barely aware of Hairydog whirling around him in excitement.

He reached Thora, and grabbed her by the arms.

'What happened to you?' His words came out in a croak.

She shrugged, but Oddo stared at the bruises and scratches on her face.

'When we crashed through the gate, I fell off. The next thing I knew, Father Connlae was bending over me. He guessed I'd go to the fort and he was waiting for me outside. Don't worry, these don't hurt any more.' She pointed to her scratches. 'I've dosed myself with herbs.'

Oddo began to chuckle, and he felt as if he'd never stop laughing. He took Thora's hand and began to pull her towards the market.

'Wait! Captain Snari's there. He'll see me and . . .'

'Who cares?' chortled Oddo. 'He can't do anything. I'm Oddo the Wind Master, remember! Come on.' As they crossed the empty market square he looked round for the Captain. 'Hey, Snari!' he called. 'Catch!' He pulled a gold bangle off his arm and tossed it into the air. 'That's for my friends. Thora and Father Connlae!'

He and Thora exploded into shouts of laughter, and even the priest seemed to understand the joke. He was chuckling as they seized his hands and, half-carrying him between them, raced towards the ship.

Dúngal danced up and down at the sight of them, and Thora leaned over the side, gaping at all the treasures in the hold.

'You've got enough riches there to pay taxes to King Harald every year for the rest of your life!' she exclaimed.

'Oh no,' said Oddo. 'That greedy swine is not getting his hands on any of these.'

'Then . . .?' Thora looked at him, her eyes wide and questioning.

He beamed and nodded.

'We've got a ship now. We can fetch our families, and go where we like!'

'To the Land of Ice!' whispered Thora.

'To the Land of *Fire*!' said Oddo.

ᛈᛁᛁ ᚢᛗᛁᚲ ᛋᛁ

31

Stormrider

'But you're going to take me home first, aren't you?' asked Dúngal anxiously.

The other two turned to look at him blankly.

'I . . . forgot you wouldn't be coming with us,' said Oddo.

'What do you mean you *forgot*?! That's what we came here for!'

'I know. But so many things have happened; we've been thralls together and everything. It'll feel funny leaving you behind now.'

'Dúngal, of course we'll take you home, if you want,' said Thora. 'And Father Connlae too.'

'It'll be easy getting home in a real ship,' said Oddo, 'after that eggshell of a curach!'

Dúngal caught Thora glancing at him anxiously.

'Dúngal was really clever to make that boat,' she protested. Then her face changed as Oddo and Dúngal burst out laughing, and she realised she was being teased.

'Come on, what are we waiting for?' She leapt over the side of the ship. Dúngal started to follow, but Father Connlae stopped him.

'It is time to say goodbye.'

'But . . . aren't you coming with us?'

'No, my child. I have met some Brothers who are travelling to a new monastery, and my place is with them. But thank you for bringing me home to Ériu, and blessings on each of you.' He placed a trembling hand on Dúngal's head.

'Father Connlae's not coming,' Dúngal called to the others.

Oddo and Thora hung over the side of the ship and the priest lifted up his hand, resting it on each head in turn. Then he bent down and patted Hairydog. When he straightened up he was smiling, but there were tears in his pale blue eyes.

'Farewell!'

A few minutes later, the three friends were cheering with excitement as they sailed out of the Liffey and back into the sea.

'Not far now!' said Dúngal.

They bounded south along the coast, the high prow rising and falling, the little ship dancing on her way.

'Hey, what's the name of this ship?' asked Thora.

Dúngal and Oddo looked at each other.

'I forgot to ask,' said Oddo.

'Then we'd better name her. How about *Gannet*?'

'No way!' said Oddo, shuddering at the memory of his last shape-change. Then his face broke into a grin. 'How about *Stormrider* – and I'll whip up a storm to drive her home. Hold tight!'

They all hooted as the wind roared, and they flew across the waves.

'Look at that sea!' shouted Thora, as the white crests foamed and crashed around them. The sail stretched and the rigging sang. 'Watch out, here come the Stormriders!'

Hairydog, in the bows, barked excitedly at the spray. But Dúngal frowned. The little ship was heeling too far over.

A moment later, she seemed to stagger, and the sea spilled through the oarholes. There was an ominous sound of water slopping under the deck. Instead of rising and falling with the waves, *Stormrider* began to lurch sluggishly.

'What's happening?'

Dúngal leapt into the hold, and to his shock he landed with a splash. Icy water swirled around his ankles. With this weight rolling inside her, no wonder *Stormrider* was so ungainly! He grabbed a floating gold dish, and began to bail.

'Come on,' he yelled, 'help me.'

Oddo dropped down beside him. Another wave pounded the ship and they both watched in dismay as seawater gushed between the planks.

'We're leaking!' As the ship tilted, they saw a crack of daylight between the planks. 'There's the hole!'

Dúngal grabbed Oddo's sleeve. 'Oddo, stop the wind. We'd better head for shore before we sink.'

Thora's anxious face peered down at them.

'You can't land here. It's too rocky.'

Stormrider heeled again and the boys were thrown across the hold. Dúngal toppled over the heap of furs, and landed in the water.

'Bail!' he yelled.

Thora was beside them now. She snatched up a jewelled chalice and filled it with water, but her arms trembled as she tried to lift the heavy weight up the high side of the ship. The next moment, she fell backwards, the water pouring over her head as *Stormrider* listed again.

'This is useless,' she yelled. 'We've got to fix it. Oddo, you plugged all the holes in *The Cormorant*, why can't you fill this one?'

'How'm I supposed to get to the outside of the ship? Didn't you notice, we're in the middle of the sea?!'

'Just mend it from here!'

'That won't work.'

'Try!'

Pressing his lips together, Oddo hacked a handful of hairs from one of the furs. With the tip of his dagger, he stuffed it into the hole.

'Here comes a big wave!' warned Dúngal, peering over the side.

They all watched as the wave hit the ship. Dúngal held his breath.

'It's working,' yelled Thora. Then the hairs showered out of the hole and the sea poured in.

'Told you!' bellowed Oddo, as they all slid across the tilting ship.

Dúngal cracked his head against a wine keg, and struggled up, tears smarting his eyes.

'I didn't travel all this way just to drown,' he raged. 'I was nearly home.'

'Can't *you* fix it?' said Oddo. 'You made a whole boat!'

'I could if it was a curach.' He slapped the wet furs. 'I've got all these hides. But . . .'

'Hey, you can swim,' said Thora.

'So?'

'That means you can get to it from the outside. *You* can fill the hole.'

The sea surged and *Stormrider* listed. This time, she didn't straighten.

'All right.' Dúngal stood up. 'Give me some fur.' He smashed the top off a clay jar, and poured seal oil over the hairy strips. 'This'll make them a bit sticky, and more waterproof.'

When he tried to clamber out of the hold, his oily fingers kept slipping on the wood. Oddo and Thora hoisted him up till he was poised on the edge, his legs dangling. Thora passed up his greasy bits of fur, and as the ship rolled and bucked, he struggled to hold on with one hand.

'Poke something through the hole,' he panted, 'so I know . . .' He lost his grip and slithered over the side.

The sea grabbed him, sucked him away, then flung him against the wooden hull. He felt as if every bone in his body was smashed, but somehow the fur was still in his fist.

'Oddo, stop those waves,' he yelled.

He thrust his face into the freezing water. Somewhere, below the waterline, he should see a movement that would show him the hole. He squinted his eyes through the salty green murk.

'Come on, Thora, come *on*!' Bits of the fur kept slipping out of his grasp. 'Hurry!'

He glimpsed a flicker below him. Diving under the water, he groped blindly forward.

'Oww!'

A brooch pin stabbed him in the hand. He thumped his fist against the side of the ship. The spike dropped back out of sight. Then, as fast as his fumbling fingers could manage, Dúngal stuffed the strips of hide into the gap. He waited for a moment to see if they would stay in place. He was trembling with cold, and he could feel

182

the sea pressing around his head, thrusting into his ears, into his nose, filling him with water. He gave one last prod at the fur, then kicked with all his strength. Up, up . . . He burst through the surface and gulped for air.

'Is it working?' he yelled.

There was a long pause, and he paddled frantically. Then Thora's head appeared.

'You've done it!'

A rope snaked towards him. Dúngal caught it and felt himself hauled into the air. He rolled over the side and crashed onto the deck.

'Keep bailing,' he gasped. 'If we don't get the water out, we could still sink.'

He flung off the fur that Thora was trying to wrap around his shoulders, and dived into the hold. The water was up to his knees.

'At least you've stopped it coming in,' said Oddo.

From the deck, Hairydog barked encouragement as they scooped and poured.

At last Dúngal straightened up and rubbed his back. 'That'll do!' The floor was still wet, but water was no longer swirling around their legs, and *Stormrider* was once more riding lightly on the sea.

'Okay, Oddo, how about a nice, strong wind. Let's get going again!'

The three of them scrambled on deck as the ship surged forward. This time, when Thora held out a fur, Dúngal snuggled inside it.

'Dúngal?' Thora's fingers played with the fur, ruffling it the wrong way. 'Do you have to stay in Ériu? Couldn't you come back with us?' She patted the fur smooth again. 'You're a Viking now.'

'Yes! You're my Viking brother, remember!' said Oddo. 'We'll buy you from Grimmr and set you free.'

Dúngal looked at them.

'You could live at our house,' said Thora. 'There are so many people there, nobody would notice an extra one!'

'No, come to my house,' said Oddo. 'I haven't got any other brothers. Or sisters.'

'Thank you,' said Dúngal. His voice came out in a funny rasp. He tried to swallow, and his throat seemed too tight. 'I . . . belong here, though,' he said.

He rose, and went to lean against the bow.

'We're nearly there!' he shouted. They had reached the yellow sandy beaches. There were the fishing nets, and . . . 'Slow! Slow!' he cried. He shaded his eyes, squinting into the glare of the setting sun. 'It's . . . It's . . . *There!*' He pointed triumphantly to the mouth of the river. As they turned, it seemed as if they were heading into a river of fire.

'Is it far?' asked Oddo.

'No!'

As the sun sank, he searched frantically among the dark shapes along the bank.

'It's getting dark,' said Oddo. 'We've got to pull over.'

'Wait!' begged Dúngal. 'Just a bit further.'

But at last it was too dark to steer. Drooping with disappointment, Dúngal followed the others onto the riverbank.

'Careful, don't slip!' warned Thora. 'This ground's all squelchy.'

'I know,' growled Dúngal.

He dozed fitfully, too excited to relax. At dawn he felt a soft drizzle pattering on his face.

Oddo stirred, opened his eyes, and frowned at the sky.

Dúngal clapped a hand over his mouth. 'Don't take away the rain,' he pleaded. 'Not yet.'

Thora and Oddo groaned and pulled their furs over their heads. But Dúngal sat up and let the moisture gather in his hair. He breathed in the sweet scent of wet earth, and listened to the dripping of the trees behind him. Somewhere in the distance, a plover whistled.

'This is Ériu,' he whispered.

As the sky lightened, he scanned the familiar landscape. Figures were already moving in the fields, and in the distance he could just make out the pointy peak of a thatched roof above the round wall of a ringfort. His belly turned over with excitement. Maybe that was his own house!

'Can Oddo stop the rain now?' asked Thora. 'I'm getting cold and wet.'

'All right.'

'Before we go, I think we should light a fire, to warm up.'

Dúngal looked at her in horror.

Thora laughed. 'Don't worry. I was just teasing.' Wrapping her muddy fur around her shoulders, she clambered on board. 'In the Land of Fire, when we get cold, we'll be able to hop in a hot lake!' she said.

As they set sail again, Dúngal watched from the bows, tense with anticipation. They rounded a bend and he shouted as Finán mac Taidhg's ringfort came into view.

'The next one . . .'

And there it was! He could see the grove of oak trees, the pink sow with the black patch rooting for acorns and, between the tree trunks, the stubbled fields and grass-covered wall of a ringfort.

'There it is!' he shouted. 'I'm home! I'm home!'

He realised Thora was standing beside him and grasped her hand.

'There's Eithne.' He pointed excitedly to his sister in her pale green léine, stooping among the trees to gather kindling.

At that moment, Eithne raised her head and caught sight of the ship. She screamed, dropped her bundle of sticks, and scurried away.

'Eithne!' he cried. But she didn't listen. 'Stop!' Banging his fist in frustration, he saw all his kinsfolk rush in panic towards the ringfort. 'They think we're Viking raiders,' he wailed.

Before the ship even touched the bank, Dúngal was over the side and racing after his sister. But as he burst out of the trees, he saw that once again he was too late. The ramp was already hauled out of sight. He ran to the edge of the ditch, yelling at the top of his voice.

'It's me, Dúngal. Look!'

The gate slid open a crack and a cautious head peeked out.

'*Dúngal!*'

There was a squeal. The gate flew back and his whole family crowded forward for a sight of him.

'How can it be you? The Vikings took you away!'

'I escaped, of course,' grinned Dúngal. 'And now, if you put the bridge back, I can come home.'

ᚾᛁᛒ ᚠ ᛁᛜᛟ ᛏᛁᛗ...

32
Gyda's secret

'We're only two Stormriders now.'

Oddo and Thora fell silent, not looking at each other.

'At least we got him home,' muttered Thora. 'That's what he wanted.'

'In the beginning,' said Oddo, 'I didn't even like him. But now . . . I'm going to miss him every day.' His words ended in a squeak and he rubbed his eyes with the back of his sleeve.

The ship grazed the bank.

'Watch where you're steering!' said Thora. 'We don't want to wreck this ship before we get home!'

'We don't want to wreck it before we get to the Land of Fire!' said Oddo. He straightened his back and frowned fiercely. They were nearing the river mouth. He steered carefully as *Stormrider* bucked and rolled in the rough water, and then they were out in the open sea.

'Right. Now, a nice strong breeze. And . . . home,' he said. He tied the steering oar in place, leaned back against the mast, and crossed his arms.

Thora grinned and joined him. 'So, are we still going to Gyda's on the way?'

'What for?'

'You know. To fetch my silver, and . . .'

Oddo let out a muffled snort. 'I don't think we need the silver any more!'

They both looked at the booty piled in the hold.

'Well, what about, you know, asking about the night we were born?'

Oddo made a face. 'I don't think we should.'

'Why not?'

'If you found out that your family wasn't really your family, what would you do?'

'What do you mean?'

'Well, would you tell your parents? Would you swap houses – and families? Go and live in the right one?'

'I . . .'

An image of Oddo's neat, clean house flashed into Thora's mind. Sigrid doing the cooking, peace and quiet, no more embarrassing moments because she couldn't do magic . . . But, what about Ketil and Harald and Sissa and . . .?

'No, of course I wouldn't go. I couldn't leave my family. They *need* me!' And then she stopped, startled by her own words.

'Exactly! They don't need another spellworker in the house messing around with magic – they want *you.*'

Thora grinned. 'Last year, when they had to pay the taxes, they would have got thrown out of the house if it hadn't been for me.'

'And I'd never leave my family,' said Oddo. 'What would Father do without me? I use magic to help with the animals and make the crops grow and everything.'

'Well, forget Gyda then. Let's just hurry up and go home.'

'So, you don't want to know what happened the night we were born?'

Thora shook her head. 'Who cares? Where we are now is where we belong.' She grinned. 'I guess that's why Dúngal wanted to stay in Ériu. With his family. Do you think we'll ever see him again?'

'Why not? We've got *Stormrider*. And I'm the Wind Master. We can go anywhere we want.'

'We might see the Sídaigi again,' chuckled Thora.

'We'll take our families to the Land of Fire. We'll show them the boiling lake and the burning ice.'

'And we'll build new houses, where there's no king and no taxes!'

'We could visit other lands, too.'

They turned to gaze across the sea. Somewhere, out of sight, there were more strange lakes, and mountains, and people. And magic . . .

♪

The Futhark

To read or write words written in runes, you have to go by the *sound* they make. These are the rune sounds:

⊬	f	∫	i (as in *it*) or i (as in *ice*)
↑	oo or u (as in *up*)	⊬	p
⊦	th	⋎	z
⊧	a	⋝	s
⋊	r	↑	t
⋞	k	⌾	b or v
⋈	g	⋈	e
⊦	w	⋈	m
⋈	h	⋈	l
⋈	n	◇	ng
⫠	ee	⋈	d
⋝	j or y (as in *yes*)	⋈	o

Can you work out why the alphabet is called the Futhark?

Writing your name in runes will give you some magic powers, but the Futhark doesn't match the English alphabet exactly. Some English words can't be written in runes.